# The Insidious Vine

tales from the archetypes:

Volume 1

'The Novice'

By

Paul Ogden

*'For what is truth but the point of view
from which you choose to view the universe'*

*Dedicated to the Pixie*
*And to all who Work in Love*

To Ardnas Yelkub

Lots of Love

Lu ap Nedgo

# Table of Contents

**Part 1 – The Insidious Vine**                    1

Chapter 1: The Child                               4
Chapter 2: The Girl                               19
Chapter 3: The Boy                                35

**Part 2 – The nature of the Vine**               50

Chapter 4: The Evangelist                         52
Chapter 5: The Curator                            65
Chapter 6: The Bright Young Things                83

**Part 3 – The Presence of the Vine**            102

Chapter 7: The Sailor                            104
Chapter 8: The Philanthropist                    122
Chapter 9: The Councillor                        138

**Part 4 – Managing the Vine**                   152

Chapter 10: The Pastor                           155

**Part 5 – Living with the Vine**                168

Chapter 11: The Lovers                           169

**Conclusion – Understanding the Vine**          186

# Part 1 - The Insidious Vine

'these are indeed the strangest of times,
bringing with them, as they always do, change and
uncertainty.
But what of the future?
Well that depends upon the degree of your perception'

It was many years ago when the vine was originally planted out in the central courtyard of the garden - in all probability on the evening of the third day during the dawning of creation. We were not present when it was initially positioned into the extremely fertile soil next to the tree, because, with the obvious of exception of the 'gardener', no other living being existed. It is a living testament to that 'gardener', that to this very day, the vine remains in good health, growing aggressively all over the world.

We can't say much about the heredity of the vine. We only became aware of its existence much later when our universal mother, Eve, in an attempt to quench her insatiable appetite, took the first luscious mouthful of the fully ripened fruit from the tree of knowledge - for by that time the vine was already growing vigorously through its branches. As you will no doubt have realised, the courtyard where it was initially cultivated, is situated at the very heart of the Garden of Eden.

Now, with the benefit of hindsight, we could say with some justification that whilst the 'gardener' of those Eden days had immense talents as a horticulturalist, he was somewhat careless. If planting the tree of knowledge in close proximity to your ancestors can, broadly speaking, be considered bad 'man management'; planting the vine next to the aforesaid tree should be perceived as being utterly obtuse and criminally negligent. However, in all fairness to that epoch of history, this particular 'gardener' wasn't to know your distant relatives wouldn't play according to the rules and regulations set out for the harmonious habitation of all beings living within the country park he had created for them.

The vine is not poisonous, although, as you will learn, the plant's very presence in your vicinity forewarns danger, and a threat to your personal health, well-being and sanity. Whilst some of you may choose to allow the vine to remain as an abstraction contained within the pages of this book, such an action could well prove to be foolish. Alternatively you may recognise the vine as a long standing companion, one you have been cognisant of for some time, yet whose existence you have previously been disinclined to acknowledge.

By way of explanation, your central nervous system, in particular that area referred to as the limbic system, has evolved a defence mechanism to fight the contagion which surrounds the vine. It does this by denying your pre-frontal cortex the ability to analyse and accept its existence. This 'programming' works on the assumption that if you are unaware of the vine it will be unable to have any impact on your life.

Having contemplated the severity of your situation we doubt the 'programming' is sufficient to protect you from the contamination revealed through the presence of the vine. We do not believe the vine cares whether or not you know of its existence – it is powerful beyond all measure. The fact it is hiding its true intentions from you, and concealing its purpose, leaves us with no alternative but to speak. Therefore, with a great deal of reluctance, we have decided to intervene. Our purpose is simple. It is to inform you of the existence of the vine; to reveal its true nature; and provide you with clues as to how you might fight the corruption which encompasses it.

But first, let us deal with the question of trust. Who are we and why should you believe in what we tell you? Well to be honest, which of course we are, although you may be able to hear us and feel our presence, you will not be able to see us. The best approximation to our substance is more than adequately described by your philosophers. They defined us as 'archetypes'; the product of your collective unconscious. As such we have existed since the dawn of your time. We exist because of you. Every action, thought and emotion humanity has ever experienced is contained within our being. As such we have come to the conclusion that it is our duty to reveal your ancestral relationship with the vine.

So within the following pages we will tell you a story based from our experiencing of the lives of some disparate individuals. Obviously, we were acquainted with each and everyone of them throughout the period they resided on this planet. Whilst each person would have wished to be considered somewhat special, unique, and in full control of their actions, their existence was intrinsically determined by the conduct of each other courtesy of the contamination associated with the presence of the vine. Inevitably, behind the beauty which individual life brings, you may feel some sadness from the reading of our observations. Let us emphasise that we are recounting their life stories so you have the foreknowledge, and the ability to develop the armoury required to succeed in your quest for a truly purposeful life. You will have skills the people you meet within the following pages did not have. Do not let our little tales frighten you, but do use the information to diagnose and determine, whether or not you are personally acting as a host for the vine.

*******************************

# Chapter 1 - The Child

> 'It is in the beginning of every life
> where there is a glimmer of hope, and,
> a longing for the new future to bring
> wealth, health, and happiness'

At the start of any story there is a beginning. In this particular narrative it commences with the Child who has already grown up before realising he is still a Child. And on one Sunday, at the beginning of a peculiarly hot spring, the recognition of this truth is proving to be as frustrating as the ongoing realisation of how ineffectual and pathetic his parents actually are.

In the Child's opinion both mother and father are extremely disappointing in very distinct and unique ways. Certainly his parents do not have the overriding sense of maturity that he has developed through the early years of his existence. Yet it was from their first and rather clumsy act of un-protected procreation during which the very essence of himself came into being within this World. The particular moment of sexual intimacy, which neither of the consenting individuals remember with any degree of lingering pleasure, is not necessarily a reason to attach blame to the parents. The Child does not overtly mind his existence in human form. No, what really disappoints is the obvious truth they possess very little intelligence in the ways of the World and share nothing in common with him. So whilst the Child has to sit through, and listen to the interminable lectures explaining the rules of engagement that go with the privilege of residence in this exacting household, he chooses not to participate in any meaningful form of dialogue with the parents. He has come to the conclusion there is extremely little he can learn from them. The Child has reached this assessment from his acute and, in his own mind, unambiguous observation of their behaviour.

On this dry sunny Sunday afternoon, within the lounge of the semi-detached house situated in the leafy suburbs of the over populated city, the Child has been instructed to sit quietly indoors with the parents. It is during this period of gentle contemplation he finds himself seeking shelter from the cross fire from yet another one of his parents "habitual' discourses.

"All I want is to be loved," the mother suddenly cries out for no apparent obvious reason.

The mother is lying on the rather old, dilapidated sofa, dressed in open pyjamas with an embroidered purple house coat wrapped over her shoulders. There is a blue, Irish Aran stitched woollen throw covering her legs. Her feet, which are poking out from under the blanket, are housed within an elegant pair of velvet green house shoes.

She raises her right arm and places the back of her hand against her forehead, takes a sip of liquid from the glass held in her left, and glares at the father.

"It's not asking for much is it, to be loved - the mother of your child. Why can't you look at me when I am talking to you?"

The father appears to have been anticipating an outburst of this type and nature.There has just been a protracted period of silence in which, with a deepening sense of foreboding, he has begun to sense his wife's customary descent into a downward spiral of overwhelming negativity. As he becomes locked within his own particular gloomy thoughts, he has indeed stopped paying her the attention she craves.

The father hears the voice but does not dare to look her in the eye. Consequently, with an increasing sense of desperation, he turns his head further away from her gaze and looks out of the window, trying to give the impression he is thinking carefully about his reply. He has the foresight to know that this particular interaction is not going to end well.

As he stares beyond the window, across the small front garden onto the road, he suddenly senses his past stretching far beyond the horizon. In his mind's eye it appears littered with the emotional detritus of every single squalid argument they have ever had. As he recalls the overall essence of each and every confrontation, feelings of resentment, bitterness and anger unexpectedly arise in his body, creating a painful sensation as if shards of broken glass were pushing into his stomach and bowels. He is scared, inadequate, guilty and lost - paralysed with no apparent control over his immediate future. For a moment he feels even younger than the little child sitting on the opposite chair who, at this moment, appears to be staring at him resentfully. The silence lingers through an eternity of several seconds. It is only to be broken when he complies with a sudden compulsion to open his mouth.

"Love – You want love? I am not sure you would recognise love if it came and smacked you over the head with a hammer." He blurts this out with all the belligerent and supercilious qualities of a sullen teenager talking to a parent who has just told him off for some or other misdemeanour.

He immediately recognises the inevitable damage this little stream of invective will have on his hoped for afternoon of peace and relaxation. No apology will be adequate, neither will it ameliorate the predicament he has just placed himself in. He is not even sure where the words came from - they just happened to find their way unedited into audible speech, unmediated by any calm, collected, or rational thought.

The mother has the unique ability to dampen and depress the joy of any sentient soul who accidentally comes within the vicinity of her being. There is generally no specific reason for her behaviour; she just seems to enjoy random acts of thoughtlessness, especially if it places her at the centre of another person's attention and relieves any boredom she may be experiencing at the time. This tendency, together with the unfortunate belief to consider that the past was the most enjoyable aspect of her life so far, means that living with her in the present moment is pretty intolerable.

She slams down the glass she has been drinking from, and recoils as if trying to remove herself from the path of a physical blow. She glares at him and the vitriol of hate which emanates from her eyes threatens to corrode the hair and flesh from the top of his head, which, at this moment, just happens to have sunk downwards to the floor in an abject act of lonely desperation.

"So you are threatening me now; you want to hit me don't you? You bastard! Don't deny it; I can see it in your eyes. You can't hide anything from me. I know you better than you know yourself. I know the dreams you have at night – you are truly disgusting." As she speaks, the venom which can be heard clearly in the tone of her voice, drips slowly from her mouth and spills onto the floor.

"Actually I despise you. You don't have the bottle to hit me and God help you if you do. I will sue you for every penny you have got. You have nothing without me."

The Child looks on regarding both mother and father with the utter contempt he feels they deserve. He awaits for the inevitable command to go to his room immediately.

It is true that one can't generally see what is going on behind the locked doors of others. We base the majority of our suppositions on whatever the object of our scrutiny would like us to assume. This is founded, of course, on the mask of their individual and familial personality. Basically we only see what they would like us to perceive. The Child knows this instinctively. Only the Child knows the truth of the life he has been born into, and he will have to wait until the body encasing his soul is old enough to make the testament of his life.

In the meantime, he spends most of his days in the bedroom manipulating a variety of miscellaneous plastic and wooden objects into a multitude of different configurations. These objects, called toys, are supposed to keep him entertained with the minimum need for input and care from either of the parents. Every evening after he has been sent to bed his bedroom door is locked from the outside to prevent him from escaping. He will also remain periodically locked within the room during daylight hours, when either of the parents conclude he is negatively impacting on their own personal enjoyment of life. The mother also has a lock on her bedroom door fastened from the inside. During the times of day when the child is permitted the freedom to roam around the house, and there is no-one else there, the mother will invariably remain locked within her own room. This is of course unless she wants his undivided attention.

The Child's room is of a relatively nondescript nature with electrostatic blue walls, punctuated by the occasional dark scuff mark initiated from previous encounters with the furniture of former occupants. On the floor there is a nearly fitted carpet which would once have revealed a multitude of vibrant colours but which is now an innocuous brown. This brown just happens to be exactly the same shade as the ancient plasticine he is allowed occasionally to play with as a treat. There is a small single bed and a child size wardrobe, re-painted, somewhat clumsily, in a dingy off-white emulsion. Within this wardrobe all of the Child's clothes are housed. The clothes themselves are a peculiar assortment. They seem to have no regard to his age, gender or size being purchased randomly from the charity shops frequented by the father, in his rather lame attempt to save money. It is these garments which give the room its underlying scent – a sickly sweet aroma of a childhood lived with an enjoyment this Child has, as yet, no comprehension of. In the right hand corner of the room there is an antique white porcelain potty decorated with tiny blue flowers. It is into this receptacle the Child is required to relieve himself, should he need to, during those periods of time when his bedroom door is locked.

There is one picture in the middle of the wall - it faces the window, stuck on with a piece of frayed, and somewhat aged adhesive tape. This once clear tape has been stained by atmospheric exposure to a murky orange brown which somewhat reflects the underlying staleness that permeates the room. The picture itself is an old, rather tatty looking poster of a Scandinavian man with long blond hair, beard, and piercing bright blue eyes. At the feet of the man there is serious looking lion and a meek, innocent looking lamb. The man is stood under an old oak tree which has, what looks like, ivy growing around it. This picture gives the impression of having been a resident in the room for a much longer period of time than the Child has. The window which overlooks the garden always remains closed. This is in case the Child should catch a cold. Nevertheless, the Child enjoys the view from the window of the garden he is never allowed access to. The mother has explain and cautioned him - 'the garden is a far too dangerous place to play in - you might get scratched by the roses and die a horrible death.

On the Monday morning, following the habitual discourse of the Sunday afternoon, just before the father leaves for what is importantly described as his 'Work', he enters the Child's bedroom and orders him remain quietly within the room - with the curtains closed - until the father returns. The mother, the Child is informed, is staying in bed with a migraine. To ensure he complies with this 'request', the father locks the bedroom door.

The Child sits on his bed and wonders about what the mother is actually doing inside her room with the migraine. Whoever or whatever the migraine is – for it regularly attends on the mother – it insists all the curtains in the house be drawn closed whilst it is in residence. This, inevitably, includes the curtains hanging in the Child's room. The Child can't quite understand the point of this imposed darkness, as the mother rarely ever comes into the room.

The curtains are fascinating and the Child finds them curiously intriguing. They consist of alternate long stripes of heavy brown and yellow velvet, and there is a peculiar looking plant, embroidered in varying shades of green yarn, on each strip of yellow. The plant grows from the bottom hem and stretches all the way up to the top. It is formed of one long curly stem, with leaves and tendrils growing two dimensionally from left to right. Sometimes during the night, whilst lying awake in silent meditation, the Child imagines that the plant is moving – twisting and turning – trying to escape from the restricting confines placed within its presence within the curtains.

In an attempt to relieve the boredom of his confinement the Child decides to help it on its journey. He proceeds very carefully to copy the flowing outline of the plant onto the bedroom wall, around the poster of the blond haired Scandinavian man. This is undertaken with the aid of the coloured crayons and pencils reserved for the sole use of his colouring book. The Child is well aware that by doing this he is wilfully breaking one of the primary rules of the household - never to to draw or write on the walls.

Later the same day, when the father returns home home from 'Work', the 'migraine' has evidently left the mother's bedroom and he is granted automatic entry to the inner sanctum. The father is allowed to lock the door behind him. This immediate right of access happens periodically, especially after one of their 'habitual' discourses. Shortly after the door is shut and bolted the child hears a great deal of murmuring, whimpers, groans and moans. The Child instinctively knows what is happening within the mother's inner sanctuary, but ignores the sounds emanating from that bedroom, and continues with his own artistic endeavours. Eventually, as the evening turns to night, the poster on the wall is framed, rather elegantly, with the flowing leaves and tendrils of the plant. The child finally climbs into his bed and falls asleep.

Whilst you may have assumed the mother goes out of her way to avoid the child, he is actually summoned to attend on her within the inner sanctum of her bedroom on a nearly daily basis. This generally occurs during the afternoon when she is feeling bored and no longer receiving the personal attention she obtains from whoever her latest 'companion' is. This long succession of women, of various indeterminate ages, are employed to 'keep house' every Tuesday, Wednesday and Friday mornings, undertaking all the chores which the mother feels disinclined to manage herself. In reality they spend most of their mornings 'helping' the mother with some or other difficulty, only occasionally leaving the inner sanctum to prepare lunch for the Child or to do a little cleaning. Each companion is led to believe the mother is their best friend and confidante. Each companion is also led to believe their friendship is vital to the mother's continuing existence on the planet. Nevertheless, and without fail, the mother will become bored with the latest companion, more often than not because they have made some misguided remark regarding her fondness towards the 'very special water'. At this juncture the father will be instructed to find some excuse to dismiss them.

The companions, owing to the limited number of hours of their employment, can only keep the mother entertained to a certain extent, leaving a vast amount of time during which the mother could become bored. The child has proved to be the answer to this conundrum.

When the mother requires the attendance of the child she makes the request for his presence known by ringing a bell. This is followed with an expletive laden command if he does not appear as quickly as she desires him to.

The mother's room is decorated slightly more elaborately than the child's room, though with the same style of curtains hanging at the window. There is a double bed, a large freestanding antique pine wardrobe, a chest of matching drawers, a bedside cabinet, and her prized Versailles gold leaf shabby chic gilt chaise longue. The bed is covered with an olive green spread and the blue Irish Aran throw resides at the foot. Above the dark veneer of the head board there is a sculpture of the same Scandinavian man who appears in the poster taped to the wall in the Child's bedroom. However, this Scandinavian man peers down from a piece of wood - fixed on to it with nails, placed through his hands and feet. The top of the bedside cabinet is covered with a piece of stained formica bearing an imprint of leaves not dissimilar to those embroidered on the curtains. Residing on top of the bedside cabinet is a bottle of the mother's 'very special water' and a glass containing some of the liquid which has been poured from it. The Child is conscious that the water is very special as the mother had screamed out very dramatically when, once upon a time, he tried to drink some.

The mother very rarely gets dressed and remains in her pyjamas for most of the day. She is quite a striking woman, approximately 5' 8" in height.

She has an angular face topped with a mass of straw coloured hair. Most of the people who ever meet her describe her as handsome. Her most obvious feature, however, is a pair of extremely large pendulous bosoms with substantially large pink nipples. As a consequence of their size, and for the sake of her own comfort, she generally leaves the shirt of her pyjamas open, to let them swing freely and unencumbered in the fresh air. She does this irregardless of whether the Child - or in fact anyone else - is within her vicinity at the time.

The day after the migraine is in residence the Child is summoned by the mother into the inner sanctum. The Child sits on the edge of the big bed whilst the mother stares at him quizzically, clutching the glass containing some of her very special water. It never ceases to amaze her just how this little piece of offspring had come into existence within her life. After a few moments of confused consideration regarding the world she finds herself in, she gives up. All that really matters is that the Child is an interesting occasional plaything, something to periodically pass the time of day away with when she is bored. She feels no degree of maternal responsibility for the Child - that is the father's role. The father is accountable for them both. This is why he goes out to 'Work', in order to earn the money required to keep them both in the lifestyle they have grown accustomed to. At the moment, on this particular afternoon, she is worrying about the father's current whereabouts.

She demands the Child to tell her where the father is and what he is doing. This is not the first time the Child has been called on to make use of what she refers to as his oracular abilities. The request is often made on those days where she has drunk more than one bottle of her very special water, and, there is no obvious source of replenishment to be found for the current bottle, which just happens to be nearly empty.

"Go on then - tell me where he is!" She demands.

The Child looks puzzled and remains silent.

The silence annoys the mother.

"Listen you little shit - tell me where he is? Stop trying to protect him - he's a worthless, good-for-nothing bastard! You know you agree with me! I see it in the way you look at him. He deserves everything he gets."

The Child remains unmoved. She stops shouting and then calmly explains she has had a premonition that the father has died in a car crash.

The Child remains silent.

"Come on - you know I am not really angry with you, don't you? It's just you have the the ability to see where he is.......... Who is he with? What does she look like?"

Inevitably the father returns as he always generally does at exactly 5.30pm, entering through the kitchen back door clutching a supermarket bag containing three bottles of mummy's very special water. She snatches the bag off him, pulls out one of the bottles, replaces the bag on the floor, and removes the screw cap from the bottle which is now firmly held in her left hand. She fills a glass to the brim, takes a large swig of the liquid, slams the half empty glass onto the table, and turns to the father.

"Where have you been? What have you been doing?" she glares at him. "I bet you have been fucking that woman all day. She is a slut, a good for nothing whore – you know she is trying to steal you from me? - Well you wouldn't know would you, because you are a man and haven't got more than a brain cell to control that prick of yours. That's where you keep your brain isn't it. That's why you are such a dismal nothing in your life - it's because you can only think with your dick. Anyway it's not that much of anything is it, and, you certainly don't know how to control it. She's welcome to it, that's all I can say." She picks up the glass and, without pausing for breath, downs the remaining contents in one gulp.

The father's head sinks involuntarily downwards towards his chest as he groans inwardly. The mother can feel his despair - finding his obvious misery rather delightful. She laughs out aloud and glares at him triumphantly, whilst pouring herself another glass of 'very special water'.

The woman who the mother is referring is the father's direct line manager. They both work at a firm of accountants in the city. They share an office, and she just happens to be of a similar age - and un-married.

"You're a spineless shit and she's a toothless slag."

Singing these words she waltzes out of the kitchen and into the living room, clutching both glass and bottle. She collapses onto the settee and starts giggling.

A few hours later, just prior to his bedtime lockdown, the child is observing the staircase from the upper landing just as the father, with some difficulty, is dragging and imploring the mother up the stairs. The mother's brain is now so confused by the amounts of the very special water she has imbibed that her body is unable to cope with the gravitational pull of the earth. She is spluttering foam from her mouth whilst he is muttering under his breath. Small sobbing noises emanate from the vicinity of his throat. Tears trickle slowly down his face, whilst a string of mucus hangs precariously from his nose.

The father looks up, sees the Child and glares at him resentfully. In a single moment the father blames the Child for all of his woes. If the Child had never been born none of this would be happening right now.

Feeling rather confused he blurts out in a rather accusatory voice, "Yes, daddies can cry as well". He considers this to be a satisfactory excuse and apology for what the Child is currently witnessing. He passes the Child on the upper landing and manoeuvres the mother into her inner sanctum, locking the door behind him.

The following afternoon all is forgotten and the Child plays alone in the hallway at the foot of the stairs. As he trots up and down the corridor the mother appears at the middle landing. She starts singing and waits for the Child to observe her. Making sure she has his undivided attention, she then slips down the stairs, lands on the hallway floor, looks at the Child and faints, but only after telling him to fetch a pillow, together with the blue throw from the bottom of her bed, and a glass filled with her very special water. Every few minutes she regains enough consciousness to have another sip of her very special water. After she has taken a swig she looks at the Child and orders him to stay with her. Then she allows her head to fall back onto the pillow with a weary sigh. This continues for the remainder of the afternoon until the father returns home. As he walks into the hallway at which point she immediately gets off the floor and with a bright cheery voice exclaims what a wonderful game she has been playing with the Child. This was the start of many such games – the rules of which become increasingly complex over a period of time.

One of the games she develops is called 'Mummy is feeling extremely poorly'. This game nearly always occurs when a second bottle of very special water is nearly empty. The mother will ring the bell to summon the Child to the start of the game. As the Child walks into the room the mother will fling her hands back against the wall and begin moaning and frothing at the mouth. After repeating the process for ten or so minutes, she will stop and glance over at the Child to ensure due attention is being given.

"Where am I?" she whispers with a voice hoarse from all her moaning and frothing.

"In your bed," replies the Child awaiting the inevitable sequence of calls and responses.

"Where am I?" she asks again. This time there is an element of pleading beginning to colour her voice.

"In your bed in your bedroom," replies the Child.

"I don't recognise it. Where am I? Where's my daddy. I want my daddy," She starts to sob pitifully.

The Child has been waiting for this. Her Daddy had died very many years ago and she loved him so dearly that she couldn't go to the funeral or remembrance service. The Child was told by the mother, in the presence of the father, that whenever she asked where her Daddy was, under no circumstances was she to be told that her Daddy had died; the shock would probably kill her.

"He's not here." The Child plays the game well.

"Where's my daddy?" she wails as she glances at the Child "and who are you and what are you doing here?"

"Daddy's not here and I am your Child." The Child awaits the inevitable conclusion to this particular game.

"Daddy's dead isn't he? He's dead, dead, dead!"

As the mother intones the word 'dead 'her voice rises in a crescendo towards the creation of the inevitable wailing sound generally associated with grief. She will manage to maintain the volume of her 'grief' for at least half an hour. She will then instruct the Child to fetch another bottle of mummy's very special water from the kitchen.

It is several months later when another new game appears, it is called, 'where is mummy's very special water'. This game commences on the completion of any bottle of very special water which appears to be the last in existence within the house. For some reason the Child's father has taken to limiting the mother's supply by hiding it in a not too secret hiding place. The mother rings the bell summoning the Child into the inner sanctum.

"Where is it?" she says with her eyes focussed to an unseen horizon. Her voice takes on that unique quality which generally occurs when the tongue appears to be too large to fit the mouth in which it normally resides.

"Where is it you little bastard?" She shouts.

"I don't know," the Child replies.

Both the mother and the Child know this is a lie. The Child has been told by the father where the bottles of very special water are hidden. The Child has been given this information just in case the mother becomes so very angry there is no choice but to provide her with more.

The mother picks up the empty bottle and tries to fling it against the wall. It falls on the floor a couple of feet from the bed. The exertion is too much and the mother falls back comatose onto the crumpled bed sheets, mouth open, eyes shut; saliva dripping down her chin. The Child quietly vacates the room. The game will continue later, in approximately one hour.

The bell rings. The Child enters the room.

"Darling, where's mummy's special water, be a sweet and get it for me."

The Child stands silently by the side of the bed, stock still.

"Sweetie, what are you waiting for? You know mummy needs her special water. She will be really angry if she doesn't have it."

The Child remains still and looks at the floor.

" I am getting really angry now – look you little bastard, just get me the fucking bottle right now or you won't know what fucking hit you, you understand you little shit. If it wasn't for me carrying you inside my belly for nine fucking months, with all the inconvenience it caused, the pain, the sickness, just so you, you ungrateful little bastard, could make your entry into the World...."

There comes a time in many relationships when something is said and a point of no return is reached. There is a silence and within that silence something happens.  There is no sound - no words to be spoken as there is no witness – only the object on which the happening event has occurred. There is no need for explanation, the Child senses the break between the past and present deep within himself; for the moment the connection has been broken in the prevailing bond between mother and son. All is now quiet and calm. Nothing will ever be the same again. Suddenly the Child feels at peace with the situation, goes to the study, opens the bottom drawer of the filing cabinet, removes the pile of papers and fetches the bottle of very special water. He places it on the stained formica top of the bedside cabinet next to the mother's bed.

Three hours later the bell rings summoning the Child to the bedroom. There the mother starts a new game of 'Mummy is feeling extremely poorly', flinging her hands above her head and against the wall. As the moaning, groaning and frothing commences, the Child just looks on as if examining a work of art. The Child imagines the moment when the mother will stop. The Child imagines the mother on the bed with her mouth and eyes wide open, rigidly still, without the ability to ever take a breath again.

The mother notices the look on the Child's face and stops the game.

"Well what's got into you? What are you looking at me like that for?"

The Child looks upward above the headboard and into the eyes of the hanging Scandinavian – who gazes back at the Child. The Child turns towards the curtain to watch the Vine twisting and turning trying to free itself and break into the room. The Child turns slowly and looks at the mother catching the one space in her eyes which still appears to be alive, and holding the space with a knowing and growing sense of perception – smiles -

"Your Daddy's dead..."

He walks slowly out of the door not bothering to look back.

# Chapter 2 - The Girl

'There is an art to receiving
There is an art to giving
There is a way to ask
And there is a way not to ask
Above all be careful what you wish for'

The World is full of princesses; they are an abundant breed, playing in the magical gardens created in their own minds by a plague of over indulgent frogs, who, quite frankly, should know better. Within the palaces of their own creation both princesses and frogs are ruled over by 'wicked step-mothers 'who have no conception of the World that the princesses, or their frogs live in.

The Girl is a Princess – she has known this simple fact all her life because her father, the frog, has told her so - he does this every morning as she wakes up and every evening as she prepares herself for sleep. At 7.30 am, as her fairy tale bedside alarm sings out its fairy dusting of silver chimes, the father, with a smile brighter than the sun, appears at the door clutching a tray on which there is glass of cold milk and a rich tea biscuit. Every morning, without fail, he will repeat the same litany which he has etched inside his heart.

"Good morning my beautiful princess. Your frog has brought you your milk and biscuit. It's a beautiful day and now more beautiful because you are awake to see it."

Half an hour later she will be found downstairs in the kitchen, sat at the large pine table opposite the Aga cooking range, where a boiled egg and toasted bread soldiers, of equal height and countenance, await their summary execution. Every morning the frog looks proudly at his daughter - the princess.

"your soldiers await your command oh most royal and beautiful princess."

He gurgles and croaks out a tiny little chuckle as he sees her wince. He then pours himself another cup of scolding hot coffee from the red enamel camping pot which resides for several hours every morning on top of the stove. Father and daughter will remain sitting at the table for another half hour before the personal home tutor arrives to provide the daily dose of education required to fulfil the legal requirement to adequately equip the girl for life within the community.

The wicked step mother of this particular family grouping is the princess ' actual mother. She is a successful business lawyer working in the nearby city. Every morning, precisely one hour before her daughter's alarm begin their fairy tale chimes, she will leave the farm for her office, and there she remains until exactly 6.00 pm. She will then return to the farm, arriving after 8.00 pm and, most importantly, after her husband has put the girl to bed.

There, within the peace and quiet that can only be achieved in the absence of her daughter, she will eat dinner with her husband. This dinner will have miraculously appeared out of the freezer, found its way into the oven, and, when duly heated to the appropriate temperature, onto a plate strategically placed between the knifes, forks and spoons which have been set out on the wooden pine table. Silently they will trudge their way wearily through the meal, masticating the food with the helpful assistance of two glasses of red wine. She will then go to her bedroom and prepare for the same routine that will materialise inevitably into existence the following morning.

Her husband will stay up for a few extra hours working through his latest field results, jotting growth figures into an old black leather journal. This will be undertaken in his oak panelled study, sat at an solid antique oak desk, surrounded by research papers and journals, which spill off oaken book cases into untidy piles on the ancient Persian rug which covers an equally threadbare Axminster carpet. This carpet was laid down by his grandfather over a hundred years previously and is now firmly integrated within the fabric of the house. At around midnight he will retire into his own bedroom to sleep on the single metal bed and horsehair mattress - the very same one he has slept on since he was a child.

The frog is aptly named, for by some quirk of nature he has two large bulbous eyes, thick lips and a tongue which is too big for his mouth. Consequently this tongue spends most of its life protruding between his thick lips spreading saliva over the lower jaw and upwards into the thin hair of the pale ginger moustache he has cultivated below his nose. He is of short build, bulky and squat, standing at a grand height of five foot and five inches. He has bowed legs and walks with a limp - this not a product of nature but of a horse riding accident which occurred in his teenage years. Nevertheless, in spite of having what many would consider to be an unfortunate physical disposition, he is extremely good-natured and prepared to live contentedly with the demands placed on him by both his daughter and wife.

He met his wife at an Oxbridge college. He was studying genetics and she was studying law. They met one day in the library when he accidentally collided into her whilst carrying an armful of books on asexual propagation and vegetative production in horticulture. He bought her a drink in the student bar by way of apology. Thereafter they got on tolerably well as fellow student acquaintances with a shared interest in country music.

However, one morning, following an evening of intense drinking celebrating the completion of their final exams, they woke up to find themselves in bed together. To be honest (though he won't admit this to his wife) he doesn't remember much about the night they obviously spent together, only that the overall end product of their sojourn resulted in the penetration of the female germ cell by one of his sperm. It was a couple of months later that his father died prematurely from a myocardial infarction. He returned home to take over the family estate and agreed to marry the pregnant girl who would henceforth be known as his wife. The resulting foetus grew to become his one and only daughter..

The frog is proud of the 150 acre fruit farm he inherited from his father. On it he successfully grows apples, pears and soft fruit. His greatest source of pride, however, is the 60 acres of Humulus Lupulus which he grows for the local micro breweries, many of which operate within the near vicinity of his farm. Humulus Lupulus, which translates as 'wolf of the woods', will probably be better known and recognisable to you as the hop vines commonly seen decorating the bars of rural pubs. To say he is passionate about them would be to understate his obsession; outside of his daughter, Humulus Lupuli are all he lives for. He is a breeder – and his latest experimental cultivation is growing on a couple of acres in the old paddock near the farm house. When he finally releases it to market he intends this new and extremely royal variety to be named after the princess.

The following morning the princess awakes yet again to the fairy tale chimes of the bedside clock and makes her earthly re-connection to the fabulous palace of her being. The frog appears at the door holding the tray with the glass of milk and the rich tea biscuit.

"Good morning my beautiful princess. Your frog has brought you your milk and biscuit. It's a beautiful day and now more beautiful because you are awake to see it."

This utterance is made regardless of the fact that the day in question just happens to be one of those of a cold, damp and miserable variety, with rain shrouding the near horizon in the dull greyness which often greets the early morning residents of this particular countryside idyll.

The princess surveys her royal chambers. Naturally, the decor is as charming and elegant as required by a princess just entering her teenage years. She has been given the authority to design the interior in any manner she so chooses. At the moment she is going through a pink season.

The walls are clothed in sumptuous royal pink and cream striped wallpaper. The wood work is painted with a lighter pink chalk wash and the window frames in an off lily white egg shell so smooth it kisses the fingers on the touch. A refurbished Georgian dressing table, with its fancy mirror reflecting the light from the large window opposite, takes proud possession of the left hand wall. A gold gilt chaise longue lies adjacent to the bay double bed, which itself is dressed in a duck feather duvet and eiderdown. Her pillows - there are four of the fluffiest variety money can buy - are decorated with tiny pink hearts. All the soft furnishings have been chosen by the princess. She only has to ask and she receives. The previous season had been yellow - but she had become bored with that particular colour scheme very quickly. A quick word with the frog and a week later one of the frog's little helpers came and re-decorated the whole room, while she went, accompanied by the frog, to purchase the requisite soft furnishings.

Every weekday, during whatever seems to resemble term time, the personal home tutor arrives at precisely 8.30 am to provide instruction to the princess. Home schooling had started two years previously following an argument which occurred between her parents because of a very simple request she had made. She had unambiguously ordered the frog, that as a princess, she had absolutely no intention of going to The Boarding School - the wicked step mother having decided to place the princess there following her potential release from the village primary school.

The frog wanted the best for his princess and did not desire her to be unhappy in any way at all. He felt this was only right to compensate for the fact that the mother, always away from home on business, was unable to pay the daughter the parental attention she obviously needed. Anyway, he enjoyed having the princess hanging around the house - it made him feel young. The mother, who had always felt her husband's behaviour towards her daughter was both peculiar and odd, was adamant the girl should go to The Boarding School – 'you know what, you can't always have what you want'. This was her own personal creed and, as far as she was concerned, supported by her own bitter experience of life.

The argument which had ensued, resulting in the slamming of doors and a period of two weeks where the mother decided to stay with 'friends' in the city, concluded with the appointment of the Governess – a personal home tutor. Whether or not this could be considered a personal victory on the part of the princess and the frog is difficult to ascertain with any degree of clarity. The mother, of course, had not managed to get 'what she wanted'. She intuitively knew that the daughter was being spoilt beyond the standard norms of life. In reality all she really wanted was the girl to be placed outside the forefront of her cognitive awareness on a daily basis. The very slight feeling of guilt she felt about her lack of maternal consideration towards the princess was more than compensated by the thought it was going to be her hard earned income which would pay for the reputable and prestigious school she had once attended. The prospect of having the spoilt brat continuing to live in close proximity to her, especially when she thought she had got rid of her, at least during term time, was a pretty bitter pill to swallow.

Naturally, it is the princess, with her own peculiar romantic fairy like idealisation of the world, who likes to re-imagine the personal home tutor as the 'Governess'.

The 'Governess' is a lady of diminutive stature with short black hair and piercing dark eyes. She is bright and intelligent, with a daughter of her own. By proxy the daughter has become the 'personal companion 'to the princess and shares in the daily lessons provided by her mother. She has become the princess 'constant attendant and confidante and fulfils whatever task the princess asks of her. This is because the 'Governess' is a consummate player of a good bread winning situation when she sees one. She has instructed her daughter she must always do whatever the little brat wants her to do. With this tidy contractual arrangement in place the 'Governess' feels sure they will be in constant employment for several years to come.

Lessons start on the arrival of the 'Governess' and finish at 1.30pm. They are held in the drawing room unless they are going on field trips around the farm. After lessons the Governess stays on doing odd jobs around the house whilst her daughter, as instructed, plays with and keeps the princess amused and entertained. At this point the drawing room becomes the princess 'personal chambers.

It is a bright, airy room with large Georgian windows looking out over the lawn. At one end of the room there are four three seater sofas arranged in a square around a large rococo coffee table. At the other end of the room, placed alongside the large open fire, is a 16 foot walnut dining table. It is at this table the students sit whilst the 'Governess' teaches. In the left hand corner of the room, close to the window, the frog is successfully growing a jasminum polyanthum. It currently stands at eight foot two inches in height with its long elegant stems tracing up the stand-alone trellis towards the ceiling. At the moment it is covered in small star shaped flowers which exude a sweet, though slightly sickly, perfume into the air. The frog is especially proud of this specimen, for as he rightly points out, this particular form of vine, originating from China, when grown indoors requires the extreme perseverance of its carer to remain healthy and full of vitality.

Whilst the drawing room is the domain of the princess during the day, at any other time, especially when the 'wicked step mother' is in residence, it is strictly out of bounds. Although the princess doesn't yet realise it, everything in this room, with the exception of the jasminum polyanthum, has been ordained at the behest of the mother. The room is designed for her own personal comfort during the weekend periods of recuperation, required to relax the mind from the demands of her business within the city.

The princess is fully aware of the imbalance of power between her and her fellow student. She sees herself as employer and pay-mistress general. Simply, if it wasn't for the princess the 'Governess' wouldn't be able to educate her own daughter. Because of this the princess feels it is only natural, and appropriate within the overall scheme of her life, to practise and hone the skills required to have absolute power over another living being. Consequently, and having been ordered to do so by the 'Governess', the attendant dutifully attends to every personal whim and need of the princess; running errands, fetching glasses of milk, brushing hair, applying make-up, massaging an aching back, rubbing oil into sensitive feet, and generally ensuring the princess receives the inordinate amount of personal validation required to convince her she is indeed truly gorgeous and admired by everyone within her own peculiarly small world.

Nevertheless, the weekends witness a certain amount of constriction and curtailment placed on both the behaviour and actions of the princess. When the wicked step mother is at home it is pretty clear who the queen and absolute ruler of the household actually is. On Saturdays and Sundays you will find the princess demure and quiet, in fact behaving with a much more appropriate demeanour for one of her position. On Sundays, following the mandatory attendance for communion at the local parish church, the frog, princess and wicked step mother, displaying all the attributes required of a genteel and respectable family unit, go to the local free house/restaurant for a Sunday roast. The Aga in the kitchen is seldom used for anything other than the coffee pot, warming toes and heating up pre-prepared meals – for the mother considers she has neither the time nor the inclination to cook because, as she would frequently state,' there are more important things to life than slaving over a hot stove'.

Every other weekend the 'Uncle' stays over. The uncle is someone extremely important at the offices where the wicked step mother works. He is not a real uncle but has known both father and mother since their days at university together. The princess is very fond of the uncle, he is tall and handsome, smiles a great deal, and, most importantly, makes the princess laugh. What she especially likes is the fact he treats her as an adult - so unlike the wicked step mother and the frog who still insist on treating her like a young girl. Even the wicked step mother is more tolerable to be with when the uncle is around. If ever there was a prince charming, the uncle, with his sports car, represents the ideal candidate. The princess dreams of him frequently and imagines the one day he will whisk her away to a new palace and a life free from the wiles of the wicked step mother. Regardless of what anyone else may think she knows that sooner or later this will happen. All she has to do is wish strongly enough and eventually make her intentions known.

All in all it has to be said that up until now the princess has led a charmed life. She has everything she needs - all the latest technological fashion accessories, watches, jewels, handbag, make up, perfumes and friends to call on. Well to be more precise, friends whom she can commandeer to call on her.

Maybe it was this charmed existence which resulted, one morning, in a sudden attack of personal insecurity. This assault on her senses started while she was contemplating her relationship with the personal companion. She asked herself." Does my personal companion really like me?"

Very quickly she came to the conclusion that, in all probability, the companion only pretended to like her because the Governess had told her to. In a sudden and most startling epiphany of revelation it dawned on her that life was too easy. She always got what she asked for. She wondered what would happen if she stopped asking – would she still get what she wanted? Would her friends bother to contact her, or even be friendly anymore?

Entertaining a certain degree of illogical reasoning, she decided she should actually no longer ask for anything. If people truly loved her all she had to do was wait – say nothing – if her 'friends 'wanted to play with her they should get in touch with her. Why should she offer herself up to others if they didn't ask first? If they didn't ask her to play then they obviously didn't want to play with her – they didn't care. She immediately proceeded with her experiment and waited to see what would happen. It wasn't long before she came to the inevitable conclusion her 'friends ' really didn't care much about her at all.

Shortly after this realisation had taken hold of her she decides to confront her tormentors by visiting them at the local village playing field. She sees the people who used to call themselves her 'friends' and walks over towards them. They smile at her, but she is not fooled. They don't care, they never have cared, and they never will care for her.

"Where have you been? 'her once upon a time playmates ask, "We have missed you."

"You didn't miss me, you never call and ask me out," the princess replies.

"We missed you – we like playing with you," they say.

"Obviously not that much or you would have called me," she replies.

"You know we meet down here every Saturday, you are always welcome to join us."

"You will need to invite me, call me." She pushes her little nose up into the air, turns away and walks up the lane from the playing field back to her house. She waits and waits for the call. It never comes so all she can do now is to consider herself friendless and unloved.

Within a very short period of time she goes from being a very happy little princess to a rather grumpy, dumpy, sulky girl, who sits during the quiet afternoons in the drawing room, sighing and contemplating how, in so many ways, her life is truly awful. Even the companion can see no point hanging around with the girl in this state and goes off to help her mother with the cleaning chores. So there, on her own in the drawing room, the girl sits in a morose and pitiful state. This continues for a whole five days at which point the frog decides he has no choice but to intervene.

The frog is not unaware that something has seriously affected the princess 'humour. It bothers him and he thinks of little else as he tends the experimental Humulus Lupulus in the two acre paddock. He comes to the conclusion that he has not presented her with a gift of any particular value for some time. What she needs is a very special gift. But what could the princess who has everything and anything want or need? It is a dilemma which the frog considers for several hours and well into the night. Finally, he realises there is no choice; he will have to tell the princess of his intentions to purchase the gift and ask her to state her heart's desire.

The following afternoon he enters the drawing room where she is reclining on the couch with her right arm flung over her forehead. She is trying to console herself by acknowledging the turmoil of her own tortured mind - recalling the many injustices she has suffered during the course of her short and troubled life. Nobody is ever going to understand her misery, especially the frog. She looks at him with a degree of annoyance – she didn't wish to be disturbed. Nevertheless she listens to what the frog has to say. As he tells her he wants to give her a present to cheer her up and that she can basically, within reason, have whatever she wants, her face lights up in excitement.

"I want a horse," it comes out of the blue, she has never previously shown interest in animals of any shape or nature. Why on earth would she want a horse?

"I want a horse. I am a princess and princesses should have their own horse on which to explore their lands. I will love my horse and my horse will love me in a way no-one else will until my prince comes." She turns and looks at the frog expectantly, preparing to perform the perfunctory squeal of extreme excitement and delight.

"I am truly sorry princess, you can have anything but a horse." The father can't believe he is having to refuse his daughter, especially after he had promised she could have whatever she wanted.

"You said I could have anything, I want a horse. Only a horse will make me happy. I need a horse. My life will be ruined without a horse. We have a farm with stables why can't I have a horse?" She stares at the frog challenging him to refuse.

"I am not prepared to allow my princess to have a horse. It is too dangerous and I cannot allow you to do anything which might hurt you."

He speaks very slowly and deliberately trying to make his point in a reasoned way.

"How dare you," she screams. "How dare you refuse me! Don't you see how much you are hurting me? You are useless! You say you love me but you are just like all the rest. You don't care or else you wouldn't be so cruel and wicked. All I want is a horse and you can't provide it. Mummy's right about you – you are a loser." To be fair she had never heard her mother call her father a loser, but it was what she imagined her mother would say to the frog in similar circumstances.

The father is all too aware that, whether she realises it or not, the princess is possibly regurgitating the sentiment of the mother's actual feelings towards her husband. He suddenly recognises a sense of loss. The princess no longer cares for her frog. Suddenly he feels a pang of pain as the knife of his future loneliness commences a slow entry into the very structure and form of his life. An overwhelming sense of sadness sweeps over him. He starts to experience a small constriction in his heart and chest as he begins to realise his little princess is growing up and doesn't really want or need him anymore.

The following morning the father does not take the milk and biscuit to the room. His soul feels heavy and troubled – he calls his daughter down for breakfast. She appears in the room with her little nose pointing toward the ceiling and her eyes focussed in any direction other than toward the father. She maintains various versions of this posture until the arrival of the personal home tutor at which point she leaves the kitchen ensuring the door makes the appropriate sound supporting her personal dissatisfaction in life. She knows she will make the father pay for his act of betrayal towards her.

In the evening, as he sits opposite his wife for supper, with the pre-prepared boeuf bourguignon which has miraculously appeared out of the freezer, found its way into the oven and onto a plate strategically placed between knifes, forks and spoons set out on top of the wooden pine table, he informs the wife of the current state of affairs with the daughter.

The wife sighs, looks at her husband wearily, places her knife and fork onto the table, takes a deep breath and starts to speak.

"I seriously believe the issue is a reflection on the state of our marriage. You know we have not been happy for some time and this is obviously having an effect on her. I told you she should go to The Boarding School. You have spoilt her and it's my fault for not dealing with our problems head on. I have waited too long to say this," she pauses before continuing. "I would like a divorce."

He looks at her in disbelief – this was not what he was expecting from the evening conversation. He places his knife and fork onto the table.

"What did you say?" he asks.

"I would like a divorce – you can hardly be surprised, we have lived separate lives for years now. I have my bedroom and you have yours. You must realise I am not happy and I deserve to be happy – I work hard enough."

An uncomfortable period of silence surrounds the table and slowly radiates through the kitchen, out through the back door and into the yard towards the paddock. The father begins to make the connections, putting together links in a fragmentary chain of unpleasant thoughts which have been floating in the periphery of his mind on and off for some time. There is the gradual dawning of realisation. This arises from the series of questions he starts contemplating and finding answers to. They all relate to the wife and uncle.

Was it not a little odd that the uncle spent so much time at the house?

Didn't they seem to spend a little bit too much time together within the drawing room having private meetings about work?

What was it they were talking about that couldn't be discussed at the office?

What was it about the peculiar way they engaged with each other, as if no-one else was there?

With an increasing state of shock rapidly taking control through his body, he comes to the inevitable conclusion the wife and the uncle are in all probability having an affair, and have been indulging in one another for some considerable time.

"This is about him, isn't it – you always liked him more than me. How long has this been going on for?"

The father can't believe what he has just said. He is not certain he can truly believe the situation he is finding himself in. Everything becomes a blur. He can no longer make any sense of his surroundings. Confusion reigns in his mind. He feels and perceives everything in the slow motion brought on by the onset of psychological trauma. The very fabric of his belief in the life he shares with this woman is suddenly shattered and irreparably broken into a thousand of tiny pieces. The yesterday he truly valued will never become a tomorrow. The present has destroyed his conviction in the values by which he has lived his life and fulfilled his duty to wife and daughter. He hears her voice as if from a distance. What she says confirms the truth.

"This is nothing about 'him'. He has nothing to do with our relationship, so you can leave him out of your equation. Obviously I have discussed this with 'him 'and he knows I have been unhappy for years. He wants what is best for me and our daughter."

This statement jolts him back into the room where he finds himself sat rigidly on the edge of his chair at the kitchen table. Every muscle in his body has tensed.

"What's she got to do with all this? You leave her out of it. She is unhappy enough as it is, there is no need to make it worse for her." He is beginning to panic.

"That's another thing," the wife looks at the husband. She pauses for the moment and intentionally allows the feeling of resentment she has always felt towards him take hold. "I am not happy about your relationship with her – there is something distinctly unhealthy about the way you fawn to her every whim. I will be taking custody as I don't think it is healthy for her to remain here with you on her own. I have spoken to The Boarding School and she will be starting there after Easter."

"What are you implying exactly?" he is beginning to sound hysterical. "Why can't you leave her out of this? How dare you make decisions about our daughter without consulting me first!"

She allows herself to become angry. She is angry at herself for living the lies that have made her life so comfortable. It had been the easy option at the time - to marry this suddenly wealthy young man because she was pregnant. She looks at him sat pathetically in his chair and feels increasingly irritated. Why can't he see their life together is a pointless sham? She suddenly has the urge to really hurt him. She wants him to feel the same sick pain that she feels during every second in his company. There has to be a point of no return. This sick little relationship needs to end right now. She wants her life back.

Suddenly sensing her husband on the verge of a complete emotional collapse she decides to bring the whole sorry episode of their life to conclusion. One final statement is all that is needed, and she makes it, with a certain degree of vitriol and more than a fair helping of spite.

"Well that is some assumption. What makes you think she is your daughter and that this was anything more than a marriage of convenience?"

She stands up from the table pushing the plate of food to one side, walks out of the room, goes upstairs to the bedroom and locks the door, removes her mobile phone from her handbag, flips through her favourites, hits the call button, and waits for the response " –I've done it," she sighs to a voice from her very near future, "I've finally done it."

The husband sits silently for a moment within a daze of confused thoughts which slowly come together to create a chain of reality that wraps itself tightly around his chest, secured with a padlock of its own making. His heart is truly broken.

The following morning the farm labourers find his body in the paddock. For some reason he has decided to rip down the experimental vines which were growing up the wires where he had planted them. The exertion was obviously too much, and like his father before him, has died from a myocardial infarction.

Six months later, on leave from The Boarding School, the girl is summoned to the drawing room where her mother and the uncle are sat drinking a coffee and eating fruit from a metal bowl containing apples, peaches, apricots and plums.

"Sit down please," the mother speaks with the tone of voice she uses to express matters of fact and importance, "your uncle and I have something we need to tell you."

The girl looks at the mother and uncle with a quizzical expression and an element of interest.

"I have found it very difficult to manage my time at the office and run the farm. There just aren't enough hours in the day and I need help. Now you know uncle and I have been very good friends for a long time – well we have decided to get married. Uncle will be moving in to help me run and manage the farm. He is going to be your new daddy."

The girl looks at her mother and then turns her gaze onto the uncle. Slowly, with a knowing smile, and a wink held secretly within her eye, she hands him the last remaining apple from the bowl.

# Chapter 3 - The Boy

'In order to exist the object needs to be observed
How well the object proceeds to exist depends on the quality
of the observation'

He walked into the classroom at the very moment the girl was explaining to a group of older pupils just how odd he was. He knows she is talking about him because her friend shrieks out that the object of her narrative is now standing behind her. "Whoops," she giggles, and changes the topic of conversation to one which equally amuses her, the house mistress 'lesbian relationship with matron.

The boy looks around the room, makes general eye contact, smiles benignly, turns and walks away, out through the door into the 'Quad 'and from the west side into the library. There in a quiet corner where he is unlikely to be seen or disturbed, he takes up a sheet of paper, chooses a selection of pencils from his bag, and starts to draw.

The 'Quad 'is essentially the school's equivalent to a cloister – four large covered walk ways formed into a square surrounding what used to be a lawn with a fountain in the middle. This is now a vegetable patch placed under the watchful care of the novice students who are using the space to grow micro-vegetables. The Boarding School – like most other schools with ancient foundations - has its own peculiar traditions. At this school – starting age 12 – the youngest pupils are known as novices for their first two years, initiates for the next two years, and superiors for the final two years. This tradition may, or may not, have been the result of The Boarding School being founded by a monastic order in the fourteenth century to instil a Christian education into the offspring of the landed gentry. Each group, i.e. Novices, Initiates and Superiors, has its own boarding house and educational complexes – the Quad houses the areas of the school which are held in common and used by all, including the main hall and chapel. It is also traditionally recognised as the oldest part of the School.

The School is set within a village in the heart of the countryside. Actually the School is the village, for the few domestic dwellings, the free-house, and post office are owned and let out to favoured tenants by the School. The sports fields – including hockey, football, rugby and cricket pitches, polo and athletic fields, surround the village in a green belt protecting the School from any encroaching development. Beyond the grounds the School owns and tenants out over a thousand acres of surrounding fields to two local farms who provide the School kitchens, there are three, with discounted seasonal vegetable, milk and pork.

The School is still firmly covenanted to the Nation's landowners, whose sons, and more recently daughters, have been entrusted to its care for over seven centuries. The School motto translated roughly from the Latin reads 'You will be valued by what you contribute to society 'Over the last forty years, just to prove this point, an equal number of its alumni have become some of the country's more prominent and recognisable politicians, all of whom have achieved the highest offices of state. Most of its other alumni are equally successful becoming the leaders of industry or heads of the civil service. The Boarding School has also produced its fair share of professional sports personalities – obviously in the more respectable sports of cricket, athletics, rowing, and, rugby. It is renowned for academic excellence, and the majority of its pupils (92% according to the brochure) go on to achieve first class honours degrees at the country's more reputable and respected universities.

Naturally the demand for places at this establishment is extremely high. However, if you want your child to attend this School you will need to fulfil one or more of the following entrance criteria. Namely you will need to ensure that: (a) you went to the School as a child; (b) you nurture a child talented enough to win a bursary; (c) you are wealthy and register your child before consummating your marriage. If you cannot get your child a place through (a), (b), or neglected to register the child before conception as suggested in (c), there is always option (d), ensure you are fabulously rich and famous, and prepared to allow your name to be used within the marketing and public relations machinery of the School. You will also need to be willing to pay an additional sum of money by way of a large charitable donation over and above the normal yearly fees, to the School's Foundation Trust.

The boy fulfilled entry requirement (a). Both his mother and father had attended the school, albeit at different times, and had determined, on a pre-nuptial basis, that any offspring of theirs would be educated there. He is an only child. As far as his parents were concerned having a child was a rite of passage to ensure the brilliance of their genes could be passed on through eternity to the following generations. They also considered the production of an heir or heiress would provide them with an increased air of maturity which would assist in the validation and promotion of the business they were developing. Unfortunately, both of them were also of the opinion that having undertaken the trials and tribulations of becoming parents they had no further familial obligations to their son other than to ensure it was fed, housed and educated. This would need to be achieved with as little inconvenience to them as possible so they could enjoy the same lifestyle they had become acclimatised too before the conception of their son. Consequently, when the boy was five years old he was sent to a prep school with close links to The Boarding School. He was transferred automatically from the prep school to The Boarding School two years ago as a category (a) pupil and he has now just entered his first year as an Initiate.

The boy is well aware he is considered as being odd – he is not deaf and can hear what people say behind his back in coded whispers. He cannot fail to observe that teachers treat him in a different way to other pupils. He is conscious that other pupils avoid him. He is aware that he is not a preferred choice as team mate for group work. On school trips the seat next to him on the bus will remain empty unless there is absolutely nowhere else to sit. If the boy cares he doesn't show it. Occasionally he will check his reflection in the mirror. He can't see anything wrong and neither would you or I if we were to meet him in the flesh. He is of average height for his age. He is neither over weight nor underweight. His skeletal system appears well proportioned. He moves around comfortably showing no sign of physical impediment. He is neither good looking nor ugly. He has dark brown hair which is neither tidy nor untidy. He dresses well but not in a way which would bring attention to himself. He is clean, acne and odour free. Maybe he just doesn't fit into the normal stereotypical view people have of the average Boarding School pupil.

At The Boarding School it is generally considered the girls should be beautiful, sophisticated, intelligent and witty - the boys should be rugged, muscular, strong and sporty. If you are neither of the above you should display outstanding academic brilliance. Arts, although their existence in the world is given a token acknowledgement, are not considered a foundational quality of the school – they are treated with a fair degree of suspicion as being a frivolous past-time encouraging weakness in character. Creatives are generally recognised as being somewhat self-centred and incapable of fulfilling the sense of public service instilled within The Boarding Schools values. As there are plenty of other educational establishment who cater for the 'Arts', the School doesn't feel any obligation to offer their study as serious curriculum options. At best the 'Arts 'can be listed as interesting accomplishments to be placed on a curriculum vitae after listing one's team attainments in the sporting arena.

It's probably unfortunate then the boy displays none of the characteristics truly valued by the School – he is not apparently rugged, muscular, strong, sporty or academically inspired. If anything he displays an unhealthy disposition towards brilliance in the art of drawing, which as indicated above, is not a talent actively encouraged or nurtured. However, the boy is not bullied in the way those of the non-sporty, academically minded pupils usually are. To begin with there is an attempt to make him a target of this particular objectionable sub-culture present in most educational institutions throughout the land. Naturally there are some pupils within The Boarding School, who, like many others before them, wish to be respected by their peers as the leaders and chief instigators with operational responsibility for all activities undertaken within this sub-culture. It is these students who, within the pursuit of the recognition they seek, grow up with a peculiar sense of temporary satisfaction from making others feel more miserable and inadequate than they are.

In their attempt to bring about a miserable existence for the boy they first try a bit of vindictive name calling, then there is some questioning about the nature of his sexuality, and finally some outright aggression on the rugby pitch. But, to the ire of his would be tormentors, he does not rise to the bait. Generally he looks at them with what can only be considered as a glance of pity, mixed with a dose of puzzled amusement, as he walks away to continue contemplating whatever he is contemplating at the moment. If his parents had given him the financial allowance they could have afforded no doubt he would have been able to buy some friends. However, in all probability he wouldn't have spent the money and it would have remained, with the rest of his meagre allowance, in his savings account. The only luxury items he allows himself is top quality 200 gram, acid free, A3 sized paper; a complete set of artist pencils and charcoals; and a soft brown leather A2 size portfolio case in which to keep his art work.

The boy's drawings are exquisite. The composition of the simplest leaves would, if observed by the finest connoisseurs of pencil sketching, be considered exceptional. He spends all his free time drawing. He does this quietly and unobtrusively as he has no particular need to be observed nor does he require any validation as to the quality of his work. He has his own standards of perfection and proceeds inexorably towards them. Neither does he choose to overtly display his talents in the mandatory art lesson The Boarding School feels obliged to place within the curriculum once every three weeks as a token gesture to those parents who feel that some form of artistic endeavour would be beneficial for their offspring.

The nominal role of 'art teacher' is allocated on a yearly basis to any teacher from another faculty foolish enough to reveal they have even the remotest artistic of temperaments. This year the role has become the responsibility of the School's highly respected rugby coach. It is felt the two hour lesson once every three weeks will not impede on the performance of his more illustrious activities within the School. Over the year this particular teacher actually notices the boy's ability but, in a rare act of kindness, doesn't draw any untoward attention to him by feeding back his own personal observations to the boy's form tutor or house mistress.

The artistic work in question can be divided into two categories – works of nature, and, works of imagination. The boy enjoys his hard earned periods of solitude hidden away within the grounds of the school sketching, flowers, leaves, blades of grass, trees, the woods he can observe perched on the surrounding hills. One of his favourite subjects is an old wizened oak tree set in the middle of the formal School courtyard garden. Climbing up this tree, defying the gardeners in its ability to survive its permanent removal, is a fallopia baldschuanica, more commonly known as a Russian vine. The boy admires its resilience and ability to grow back against all odds up the side of the tree. Over the years he has drawn the tree and vine from a wide variety of different angles. What is truly exceptional about these drawings, apart from the amazing sense of perspective they display, is their three dimensional quality – the sense you could pluck the tree and the vine from the paper and replant them in the ground.

The works of imagination are of equal brilliance. Whilst we are calling them works of imagination there is always a flavour of reality about them. These are the pictures he tends to draw when the weather is inclement. In their execution he pays them as much attention in detail as he does with his works of nature. The inspiration for these pictures generally comes from something observed and, more often than not, something felt. He has drawn three pictures this term. The first is very clearly of the girl. You can see it is her because he has captured her whole persona and physical characteristics. She looks out from the picture with her trade mark sulky demeanour, pouting her lips. He has captured her angular face topped with a mass of straw coloured hair and her gravity defying breasts. However in this picture she has her hands folded over a belly obviously extended in size through pregnancy. The second sketch is an equally obvious representation of the art teacher/rugby coach who for some reason has his arms wrapped around the lesbian house mistress 'waist. The final drawing is of a plane crash in the middle of an elaborate forest of trees. All his pictures are dated – he uses them as a form of diary – and signed off with his personal motif, a detailed representation of a vine leaf, taken from the old oak tree, drawn into the bottom right hand corner.

In the years following his initial placement in school his parents have become extremely busy and financially successful. They spend much of their year touring around the world giving lectures on this, that, and anything else they believe will make the universe a better place for them to live and breathe in. Consequently they see very little of their son as his holidays are always scheduled at the most inconvenient times of the year – essentially those times each year when schools generally have their holidays. As a result the boy spends all his vacations with an elderly lady who has the honorific title of 'Aunt'. She is not related to the parents in any way, and they don't really know her particularly well. She was a very close friend of the mother's mother and father before they died. Both sets of grandparents passed away shortly after celebrating the continuation of their biological line through the birth of the grandson. Both of the boy's parents came into the world with what they considered to be the singular advantage of having no brothers or sisters.

The aunt lives in a small two bedroom bungalow owned by the local housing association on the outskirts of the city. She has lived there for most of her life. The furnishings which make up the bulk of her possessions were new when she first moved in forty years previously. A succession of totally adored pussy cats have rendered a unique odour which will probably form an integral part of the bungalows 'fabric until demolished.

The boy spends most of his school holidays residing in the bungalow with the aunt, sleeping in the spare room which has, over the years, become his own personal space. Indeed there is a wardrobe containing some of his clothes and several of his 'works of nature 'adorn the walls. His own familial residence is in a small village situate within the countryside near the city. However, if we were to add up the amount of time he has stayed there since he was six, it would barely total two months.

He feels comfortable enough with the aunt although he does perceive her as being somewhat ancient in years. This is only natural as most children consider their parents to be old beyond belief and so therefore the next generation above the parents are considered truly antique. In reality she has only just turned sixty five. Until taking early retirement ten years previously she was a highly respected head teacher of a local primary school. She now supplements her rather paltry pension by looking after the boy during holidays and childminding four younger girls during term time for several hours a day before and after school.

Over the years she begins to see him as the child she never had. She dotes on him and feeds him home made shepherd's pie with boiled cabbage and rhubarb crumble on what feels like a daily basis. He never complains and appears to enjoy it so much the aunt doesn't consider it necessary to change the menu. Every Sunday when he is at 'home 'she takes him to a local church, the Church of Universal Values, where the elderly members of the congregation make a fuss of him, tell him how beautiful he is, and how he will break the hearts of young ladies as he gets older.

He spends most of his time in the aunt's garden doing all the chores she is no longer capable of, and, of course, sketching. There are no friends to play with because quite simply he doesn't have any. This doesn't seem to bother him in any way at all. In the evenings they sit together, she will read a book, occasionally narrating parts out aloud – he will continue with his drawing. There is no television only a radio which is occasionally turned on for the news. He has no computer, computer pad, mobile phone, or any of the accoutrements most teenagers feel they need in order to consider that their earthly existence has any degree of substance. He has never asked for any such gadgets and his parents have never considered purchasing any for him.

He arrives back at The Boarding School after the half term break to find the compatriots with whom he shares his lodgings – also euphemistically known as house mates – in a state of heightened hysteria brought on by tidings of a scandalous and salacious nature. He is mildly surprised that the girl, who would have liked to have become his chief tormentor in life (if he had been interested enough to allow it), has been removed from The Boarding School for allowing her hormones get the better of her intellectual capacity in an emotional tangle with a superior student. The result of their intimate game of mummies and daddies has resulted in the general outcome nature has provided to mark the successful conclusion of this particular sport. More surprising, probably, was the news that the art teacher (aka the rugby coach), has married the house mistress (aka the lesbian), and has taken up residence in the house with joint responsibility for the inmates.

As with all such matters the hysteria dies down and life proceeds in its daily routine with sunrise and sunset occurring every morning and evening as before. Everyone quickly forgets about the girl. Within a matter of weeks the novelty of the house mistress and the rugby coach being husband and wife wears off. The couple behave and give the impression of having been married for years. The pupils very rapidly forget there was ever a time when the two of them had not been an 'item'.

It was shortly after returning from half term that the boy was summoned by the house mistress and her new husband into their private domestic quarters, situated between the girls and boys quarters within the Initiate's boarding house. It was there, with sincere gravitas, laced with suitable expressions of genuine concern, they had to advise the boy that both his parents had been killed in a plane crash over the rain forest of Borneo. It was a small charter plane carrying six people who were travelling inland on a holiday excursion.

The boy receives the news calmly and both teachers are surprised there is no obvious emotional reaction. The boy just accepts what has happened has happened and shows no particular concern about his future. In reality as he matured into his teenage years he discovered he felt as much emotional connection to his parents as his parents displayed towards him

– which in all honesty was not of a significant amount ever likely to be missed, or subjected to any form of grief in its absence.

For the following two weeks he is conscious of being the centre of unwanted attention. Teachers are observing him closely, other student colleagues look at him with sympathy, and start whispering together in huddles after he walks past. Attempts to provide comfort and empathy fail, it's not that he rebuffs these people and their genuine approaches, he just does not know what they are fussing about. Soon they leave him alone and, slowly, his life at The Boarding School returns to normal with the one exception - in return for losing his parents he seems to have acquired a 'guardian'.

The guardian is an interesting man. He has a wife and two teenage children of the female variety. He is extremely successful at being the chairman and chief operating officer responsible for the management of the major international engineering company which he set up some years previously. He now has, following the death of his dear friend and friend's wife, the unforeseen responsibility for nurturing and protecting the life interests of their one and only son.

The agreement for him to be executor and guardian on behalf of the couple occurred during an evening dinner party. The arrangement was encouraged with the liberal accompaniment of several bottles of extremely fine white Burgundy from a vineyard in France. At the same time his friend had agreed to do the same if anything happened to him. They were young, in their mid-thirties, and didn't really think anything of consequence would ever happen to them. The agreement was more about increasing the bonds of fellowship which had commenced during their period of internment together at The Boarding School. They were considered outstanding pupils who would go on to achieve great things for society – and, in the mindset of The Boarding School, they were, and are extremely honoured alumni, frequently recalled for speech days where they can motivate and rally the existing students, to go out into the world and do likewise, by contributing through industrious labour to the ennoblement of life in that most glorious of realms within whose confines the School is situated.

The guardian, although suffering from a state of shock at the loss of his close friend, has decided to take his new role as protector of the boy's ongoing welfare very seriously. Indeed he has decided to visit the school in order to discuss the boy's future and prospects. He is meeting with the Head of the school, the house mistress and her new husband.

"To be honest there's not a great deal I can say about him, he is an odd boy, quite surprising really when you consider his lineage."

It is the Head who is speaking.

"He doesn't stand out in any way at all. He is not academically bright, just average, and he shows no interest in sport whatsoever. In fact he has no particular talent in anything that could be described as useful. No, he is not going to set the world alight. Very unlike his parents. A bit of a disappointment to the School – pupils like him."

"Well I can't see any great point in moving him on to another school at the moment, do you?" Whilst the question the guardian is posing is clearly rhetorical it still manages to generate a response.

"No, no, no, of course not. As you confirmed earlier there is no issue with fees – his parents left a considerable sum and we are really grateful for the substantial amount they bequeathed to the School foundation. It would be wrong to take the boy away from what must now be the only home he knows."

"Well, as far as his home is concerned I have spoken to the aunt and she is more than happy to continue looking after him during school holidays. Whilst I recognise I am technically responsible for his accommodation I really have no place for him within my own household. It would disrupt our family life too much – and I am not sure it would be healthy or appropriate for him to mix with my daughters. Boys can be so difficult at his age. As long as I know he is here and that you will look after him I will have fulfilled part of my obligation to his parents. Managing the actual legacy which he will inherit on his majority will be a problem for another day."

"Rest assured," the Head lowers the pitch of his voice and with a suitable sense of gravitas, marked with the appropriate timing warranted for an occasion such as this one, continues," We will be as parents to the boy as his own parents were to him."

It is agreed the boy will stay at the School until he is eighteen. Hopefully by that time he will have shown enough academic nous to gain entry to at least one of the lesser universities where he will bide his time until the age of twenty one at which point the legacy held in trust will be transferred into his own personal care. Having determined the boy's ongoing future to the satisfaction of all those present, they leave the meeting feeling justifiably proud having acknowledged the guiding principles of the School motto - by charitably taking on the responsibility for maintaining the welfare of an orphan - albeit a rather wealthy one.

As a special treat the guardian takes the boy out for lunch at a nearby countryside hotel and explains the plans which have been made for him. The boy listens in silence looking carefully at the man opposite him. The guardian begins to feel uncomfortable under his steady gaze.

"Look I am really sorry all this has happened. It wasn't my fault you know. I can't explain in words just how sad I am to lose your father - a great personal friend. But you know, life is tough and sometimes we just have to take it on the chin."

The boy continues to regard the guardian passively. He remains motionless in his seat. The guardian regards the boy - he finds his boy's behaviour disconcerting."

"You know I have to say that you are really a very lucky young man. I am not sure you quite appreciate what your parents have done for you. Take what life has given you. Don't waste the opportunity they have provided."

They finish lunch in an uncomfortable silence, the guardian pays the bill, leaves a tip, and drives the boy back to the school. After saying goodbye to the guardian, the boy goes up to his room in the Initiates 'boarding house, takes up a sheet of paper, chooses a selection of pencils from his bag, and starts to draw.

It was at 2 am one morning when a fire starts in the attic of the initiates ' boarding house. The fire service believe the conflagration started as a result of an electrical fault. The evacuation of the premises is successful and by 3 am all students, house mistress and husband are fully accounted for. No-one is hurt and temporary accommodation is found for all the students within the Novices boarding house. Naturally there is a degree of inconvenience for the Initiate students as all their personal belongings, as custom dictates in emergencies such as this, are left behind in their rooms when the fire alarm sounds. It is several days before the individual personal belongings which are not permanently damaged by the catastrophe start to be returned to the students.

The boy is called into to see the Head. The Head is sat in his oak panelled office, at a large antique desk, surrounded by photographic pictures of familial individuals at various stages in their personal development as human beings. Behind him is a large window looking out over the School grounds. The walls facing the front, and the left side of the desk are covered with portraits of previous Heads looking extremely sombre and important. These life-size representations of the past are rendered in the finest oil paints and contained within victorian style ornate golden picture frames and serve as a constant reminder to the current Head that his appointment in the role has no permanence or immortality surrounding it. The whole of the right side wall is taken up by a large oaken bookcase of the type you would expect to find in the grand old library of a stately home. Within its shelves are housed large leather covered editions of what once may have been considered important and essential works of educative literature. Now they remain in situ untouched or molested by inquiring fingers – they serve to add a soupçon of gravity to all and everything that proceeds within this hallowed space.

As the boy walks in he is ordered to sit on the large leather chair placed on the opposite side of the desk to the Head. The boy notices that the Head has his soft brown leather A2 portfolio case in front of him and is perusing through several of his works of imagination – one after the other.

"I didn't know you could draw," says the Head.

"I never thought anyone would be interested in my drawings," replies the boy. He is not intending to be provocative in his reply. He is just stating what he considers to be an objective reality.

"Well they are certainly interesting. I see you put dates on them. Would that be the date you draw them?"

"Yes," replies the boy.

The Head looks puzzled and returns his attention to the dates on the drawings which are placed next to the monogram of the vine leaf. He looks at the portrait of the pregnant ex female student, studies the date and looks at his diary. He then looks at the portrait of the house mistress and her husband, studies the date and again peers in his diary. He looks at the drawing of a plane crash and again checks the date to his diary.

"All these pictures seem to depict an actual event which took place, but events that took place after the date you claim to have drawn the picture. Can you explain how that that happens to be?"

"They are just pictures I drew from my imagination – nothing more," replies the boy.

The Head turns to the last picture on the desk. It is drawing of the boarding house, and depicted in graphic detail on the paper are flames and smoke pouring from the roof and out of the upper floor windows. The Head examines the date on the side of the picture placed next to the monogram of the vine leaf.

"William - did you have anything to do with the fire?" The Head is unsure why he is even bothering to ask such a question, but he does anyway.

The boy looks at the Head with a smile of amusement and fastens his gaze on the puzzled expression he perceives within the eyes peering back at him and shakes his head.

"Now that truly would be 'odd' wouldn't it?"

# Part 2 - The Nature of the Vine

'For some there is the food of life
For others – you are the food of life'

U nlike the majority of vegetation covering our planet, the vine we are talking of no longer has leaves, tendrils or stem visible to the naked eye. It does not need the light of the sun for photosynthesis and neither does it now require roots in order to find sustenance from the soil; for its source of energy and worldly existence is fed through the light of the living. To put it succinctly – it feeds on you.

All of you will have had experience of the vine and most of you will have felt its tendrils caress your body as it tries to inveigle its way into your life. However, you will almost definitely not be aware that any of the feelings generated within your central nervous system are related to the vine - for it is truly insidious. Within the chemistry of its own living photosynthesis, it promotes a warm sensation of comfort as you succumb to the joy of its personal feeding. The pleasure you will feel temporarily allows you to forget what reality is. This is, of course, assuming you had any sense of reality before it placed its first tendrils around the soles of your feet.

Whilst the fruit of this vine does not produce alcohol to intoxicate you, nevertheless you will become drunk through the warmth and comfort of your imagination as you sink into a way of being which encourages you to believe that everything seen, thought, heard and felt is of intrinsic benefit to you and your relationship with the universe.

In the totality of our knowledge the singularity of the vine has planted itself within every generation which has lived on the planet since those heady days in the Garden of Eden. We understand it believes in its own immortality and that it will survive beyond the end of time. At the moment its main concern is with the present generation. Whilst he past and future are an essential part of its existence; nevertheless it is in the current moment where it thrives. It has no apparent need to interpret history or to consider the future. The gateways it uses are provided through whatever is made available and revealed within the current civil mores. Each generation provides a multitude of their own gateways and the vine will always continue to make its appearance felt more acutely within the wars and other global acts of brutality, which, during the aeons of your various incarnate civilisations, there have, and always will continue to be many.

However, as we indicated previously, we do not believe the vine cares whether or not you know of its existence – it is powerful beyond all measure. However it seems within its nature to conceal its purpose and remain invisible to the naked eye. Whilst we occasionally see its shape within your media reports, it co-exists surreptitiously within whatever you are doing at this moment - whilst undertaking the natural routine and habits of your daily life. It is here where it can wrap its tendrils around your feet assisted by the reality of your innocuous thoughts and actions.

*******************************

# Chapter 4 – The Evangelist

The sign says 'Come and meet Jesus'
"Where is Jesus?" the boy asks
"He has just gone to fetch a coffee" the girl replies
"What the real Jesus – the one from the bible?" the boy asks
"Yes, that Jesus," the girl replies
"How do you know it's the real Jesus?" the boy asks
"Because I am Mary Magdalene," the girl replies

She can't remember when she started talking to Big Daddy – or indeed when Big Daddy started responding - telling her exactly what other people should be doing in their life to help her in the continuation of her earthly ministry. What she can recall is it coincided with the time she awoke in the middle of the High Street screaming to be saved – and she certainly was on this occasion.

The nice people came with an ambulance, took her to the local hospital where after a course of gastric lavage it was declared that any toxins which were in her stomach had now been cleared out. It had been the cocktail of vodka and pills she had ingested with her boyfriend over a six hour period which created the perfect conditions to be saved. And from that day on she was saved. Well to be honest she was saved on that day, and, another day, and a few more after that. She made quite a habit of being saved. And each time she was saved she would happily deny her previous 'savings 'as not being quite the real thing. What was of most importance, and the reason why she enjoyed being saved so much, was the simple fact that Big Daddy generally provided everything she needed for a relatively comfortable existence.

The evangelist likes to think of herself as a 'citizen of the World', free to roam and live where she likes and with whomever she likes at the time. Basically this equates to being' of no fixed abode'. She sleeps around, both figuratively and literally. She is bright and intelligent and once even won a place at at a major university, but neglected to take it up. She has never had a job and has never claimed any form of benefits. When Big Daddy doesn't seem to be able to provide, her parents will.

Her parents are not extremely wealthy, but rich enough and intelligent enough, in an old fashioned middle class way, to want the very best for their offspring. They are strict chapel in their religion and equally fundamentalist in their taste. They have seven children for whom educational funds were set up at birth. With a large extended family of aunts and uncles, together with their own mothers and fathers, making financial contributions in lieu of physical presents on birthdays and religious festivals, by the time each child reaches eighteen years of age there is more than enough money in each pot to cover tuition fees and basic living at a university of their choice. The fund is to be used for educational purposes only.  At the age of thirty the evangelist's pot remains un-touched.

Although they are both strict chapel by tradition, the parents live separate lives in different parts of the country. In fact about as far away from each other as is practically possible. They divorced when the youngest child - a boy - was two years old. The evangelist was the fourth offspring to be born and was eight years old at the time. In the divorce proceedings both parents cited each other as being psychologically and physically abusive. The father now lives in a large rented cottage in the north of the country whilst the mother retains the marital home in the south. This fortuitous act of generosity on the part of her parents means the evangelist has two places of refuge which she can frequently use in extreme times of adversity. This is especially beneficial as she always seems to manage to outstay her welcome with one or other parent within three months of being resident with them. Because the parents and the siblings live so far apart they rarely communicate with each other. The anecdotal stories about 'what the evangelist did next 'whilst residing in the vicinity of one of their particular neighbourhoods, rarely travelled from the south to the north, or from the north to the south.

However, as far as the evangelist is concerned living with the parents is an option of last resort – it constricts her movements and preferred habits of behaviour. The evangelist prefers to hang around small towns and cities where no-one is likely to know or notice her beyond the select group of people she is working on. Once she has established a 'position 'in a town she will return there - not frequently enough to draw too much attention to herself, but often enough to ensure a perfect harvest. Followers of Big Daddy are fully programmed to help the poor and needy, especially if they turn up at their church on a Sunday - it saves them from having to feel any guilt regarding the people who instinctively repulse their sensibility as they walk past them in the course of their daily routines. Not one of Big Daddy's followers are likely to refuse the evangelist or question her motives – well not to begin with. Quite simply, because she has invoked the name of Big Daddy, to refuse to help her would break the 'rules 'and go against the principles set out in the Beatitudes. In this way the evangelist obtains food, clothing, lodgings, use of motor vehicles, use of modern technology, and, more often than not, enough money to fund her occasional luxuries – alcohol, tobacco, and drugs.

The evangelist prefers the more informal churches – the ones where people enjoy worshipping Big Daddy by calling out ecstatic prayers motivated by the Spirit. She likes people who raise their hands in the air whilst singing praise. She especially likes the churches who encourage the congregation to share their personal testimony. She also prefers her ministers to be of the male variety. As a general observation she finds female ministers rather tricky to deal with and far less trusting than their male counterparts.

Her rules of engagement always follow the same general plan of campaign. She will decide upon a town which appears to have many active congregations. She will post a request on the internet, using one of the many chat rooms dedicated to Big Daddy. This request will generally reveal an intention to go to a town and attend whichever church she has identified as a viable source for her ongoing 'spiritual' welfare – 'would anyone care to give her a lift and join her at the aforesaid church for the following Sunday's morning service?'

Having successfully organised transport, she will arrive at the congregation of her choice at least half an hour before the commencement of the morning service. During this time she will engage in animate conversation with the pastoral team, deacons, worship leaders, flower arrangers, musicians, ministers and any friendly looking elderly members of the congregation. All conversations will be sprinkled with liberal quotes from the New Testament – suitably relevant to the topic under conversation. At some point in the service she will make a stand – she generally finds the first set of prayers a good time to interrupt the flow of proceedings. In some churches she doesn't even need to interrupt as the minister asks the congregation if they have anything they would like to share. The essential thing she has learnt over the years, is not to leave the interruption beyond the sermon. By this time the congregation are generally tired, bored, or in deep reflection.

The interruption itself normally follows the following formula. She will wait for an appropriate moment of silence – the end of a praise song is primarily a good time - especially if it one of the more uplifting variety encouraging a state of ecstasy. In the silence which follows the falling echo of the last chord, the congregation will hear a bright young female voice call out.

"Praise the Lord, for by His mercy we have all been saved. Thank you God for all you have done for me in my life. May your name be known throughout the whole World. Let the World tremble at your mercy and love."

At this point the evangelist will have stood up and moved to the place in the church where the service is being led. The congregation will then observe a young, pretty woman in her thirties, with long red hair cascading over her shoulders falling just short of her waist, wearing a long flowing multi coloured dress of the type generally found for purchase at the average folk festival. At this juncture if there is a microphone she will ask the presiding minister to give it her. The minister will be clueless about how to deal with this situation as his training did not cover the eventuality of his morning service being hijacked by the evangelist.

Holding the microphone, she will look up to heavens, and then she will begin.

"Hallelujah. Praise the Lord. For once I was a sinner and I have now been saved. Thank you God for giving me the opportunity to share your love with these wonderful people."

The last sentence is designed to ensure nobody removes the microphone from her for at least the next five minutes. Five minutes is roughly the amount of time she needs to get the full dynamic subtlety of her story across to her unsuspecting audience - a life of addiction to sex and drugs, and her subsequent miraculous conversion to a heightened state of rapturous grace. If the minister does not have the wherewithal to remove the microphone the evangelist will see an ideal opportunity to lead the congregation in flurry of ecstatic prayer.

If you were to ask her about her own personal ministry, she would explain, with tears falling copiously down the side of her face, that her calling is with the down and outs of this world, the alcoholics and drug abusers. These are the people she truly empathises with and who she has been called upon to save. And indeed, she does spend a great deal of time with them, generally in between visits to the various regional centres she blesses with her presence. She will share their vodka, pills and needles whilst giving them the Gospel. Generally by the end of a visit to one of her own special congregations she requires saving yet again.

As the morning service comes to a close she will have achieved her aim – to be the centre of everyone's attention. Inevitably someone will ask her what she is doing for lunch. Equally inevitably she will be asked where she is staying. She will reply that she has nowhere to stay and has come to the town looking for a job. The result will nearly always be the same - a meal and a bed for the next few nights.

Once she has a temporary base she can immediately start harvesting the other members of the congregation. Her aim is to get at least five 'safe ' houses she can float around on a weekly basis - preferably with full internet and access to some alcohol. Her hosts will almost always provide her with a little pocket money. If she is especially lucky the minister will be so impressed by her performance he will arrange for her to speak at local house groups, and meetings where a few people from other congregations may be present.

She is fully aware that staying at one house for more than three nights in a row is likely to cause tension between her hosts – for there are nearly always two of them. She also finds staying in one place for too long starts restricting the way she would prefer to live her life. If she is extremely unlucky she will end up in a household where they abstain from alcohol. Equally frightening are the households where she might be asked to undertake some domestic chores such as washing up dishes after she has eaten from them. Her aim is always to leave just before she has outstayed her welcome. If they have been good hosts she will return – indeed there are households where she has returned year in and year out.

Before moving from one house to another she will determine very carefully who her new host should be, taking into account the potential susceptibility to her charms and their ability to provide for her. She will consider her game plan and then turn up unannounced at the victim's abode - generally by mid-afternoon towards teatime.

Today her chosen victim is sitting on a chair in his garden drinking a glass of lemonade whilst playing on his laptop. The evangelist enters through the back garden gate, sees the victim and pauses, waiting for him to see her. He hears the gate open and looks towards her, acknowledging her existence with a wave, and what can only be described as a smile of pleasure. She places the palms of her hands together, and begins to raise them upward towards her face in a movement of prayer. As her hands go over above her head she separates them, bringing them down towards her sides in a circular movement to the left and right. It is wonderfully theatrical - she knows it, and smiles broadly revealing a complete set of pearly pure white teeth. She winks, slightly flirtatiously, at her victim.

"I was speaking to Daddy and he suggested I come over to see you – he's always right you know - bless you Daddy." She cocks her head upwards as if listening to a voice and bursts into peals of joyous laughter.

"Daddy says he has got wonderful plans in store for you." She starts dancing around in circles, giggling, laughing, singing away, "of course I will tell him."

She skips over towards him, sits down on the chair next to him, pulls out a bible from her satchel, opens it and starts reading from Paul's letter to the Romans: Chapter 12, verses 9 to 21, 'Actions of Love'. Surreptitiously the victim is gently reminded what the marks of a true follower of Big Daddy are and, most importantly, how they should be ready to provide for the need of others.

"Daddy is so wonderful – why don't people get how wonderful Daddy is? The time is coming when the whole World will know his truth and all will be saved. We are so lucky, you and me, for we know the truth already." She closes her eyes, raises her head and arms towards the sun, and exclaims in a loud voice " –Hallelujah – thank you Daddy. Thank you for my kind friend here. Bless him and let him feel your love."

She looks at her victim.

"Do you have internet access? I need to go on-line and check in with my folks to let them know I am ok."

It will be a few weeks before any congregation of her choice starts feeling slightly suspicious about her. Gradually they will begin to notice she doesn't appear to be trying particularly hard to get a job. She will have failed to go to interviews which have been arranged for her. She will not fulfil commitments she has made to the congregation, for example; to organise after service tea/coffee. She will fail to do the flower arrangements she said she would as a thank you for all the support they had given her. Most of the time they are little things which start pointing towards a larger inconsistency. This does not worry the evangelist overmuch. If life begins to get a little difficult she will change allegiance to another congregation and the whole process will commence again. The evangelist is more than aware that regardless of any protestations to the opposite, most congregations do not converse with each other in any meaningful way. This is quite simply because each congregation feels they have interpreted, and fulfil the rules established in the name of Big Daddy, more effectively than their competitors. Consequently any suspicions surrounding the evangelist will remain within the congregation she has most lately been associated with.

Eventually the harvest will be over; she will have exhausted the goodwill and energies of each and every congregation in the area. When this happens she knows it is time to move on. It is at these moments when she likes to explore her own personal ministry out of sight from the prying eyes of a Big Daddy congregation. How far away she travels and how long she stays away will depend on how much money she has managed to borrow or pilfer from her unsuspecting supporters. Nevertheless, she will return. Memories are short - and by the time she does return she will have been saved again.

In the meantime, within this most singular of towns, she has taken a very special interest in the spiritual welfare of this single man – the victim, who is sat in the garden and has just handed over his laptop, together with the requested internet access, for the evangelist to use as she wills.

The victim lives with his mother in an old end of terrace cottage at the edge of the town centre. At the tender age of 39 he is slightly older than the evangelist. To be honest he is not particularly bright but is eager to learn. What he lacks in looks, health, and physique is more than compensated by the fact that he has a large amount of money saved away for the day he decides to marry and have children. This of course will happen when he is able to escape from his mother.

He has lived with mother all his life and has never left the home, nor the town he was born in. Mother has had a hard life, having been left by her husband to look after their son on her own. She has neither the looks nor inclination to find another man to fill the big gaping hole which hasn't been occupied since her devout husband, on the instructions of his Big Daddy, left her for another woman from a different congregation. She has doted on her son – and the victim has doted and despised the mother in equal measure. He feels trapped in a mundane life, with a mundane job, with mundane prospects, and the absence of someone to share his life with on a more intimate basis.

The evangelist is the woman of his dreams, identical to the masturbation aid he has created in his mind and fantasised over for most of his life. She is beautiful, witty - in fact everything his mother can't be. His fascination started in the garden and has very quickly grown into an obsession. She has occupied his thoughts on a daily basis ever since she walked through the gate.

The evangelist had not appeared to be the type who would go in for romance. However, she begins to recognise in the victim certain attributes which are really quite attractive and interest her greatly. Subsequently she has started to pay much more attention to him than she would generally expend toward her ordinary victims. Every Sunday she can now be found sitting next to him in church, taking coffee with him at the end of church service. Then finally, one Sunday after church, she accepts his invitation to go for a roast lunch at the local inn. There they sit, eat, drink and talk animatedly until the landlady rather pointedly advises them the Inn is due to close for the afternoon. He goes to the bar and pays off the substantial tab which has accrued during their time together - the evangelist does have a taste for rather exquisite and expensive single malt whiskies. Naturally he pays up and does not ask for any contribution towards the food and drink – after all he is a gentleman and she is a respectable lady.

She re-introduces him to the world of Big Daddy in a way he has never quite envisaged before. Whilst he personally does not have the unique ability to have Big Daddy on standby to converse with at any time of day and night, she more than makes up for this particular inconvenience. She is receiving and relaying daily messages to the victim, and to be honest, life is looking good. He is turning a corner – Big Daddy has major plans for him.

Mother is not impressed with the evangelist. She has seen the change in her son and is worried he is being led astray.

"You know mum, she really is a lovely girl. Aren't we lucky to meet someone so close to God? She is a breath of fresh air. Isn't it great to have another young person in our congregation?"

The mother sighs, and places the teapot on the table, rubs her eyes with her hand and wipes them on her skirt. "You don't seem to talk about much else these days, do you now? I'm not sure about that woman. There's something funny about her. I mean what do we know about her?"

The victim winces. He has got to the rather marvellous stage of personal infatuation where any slight criticism is seen as outright condemnation of both him, his imaginative relationship, and the object of his desire.

"You just don't like it when anyone takes an interest in me or my life. You can't face the fact that someone might find me interesting and attractive." He pouts sulkily.

"Oh darling, it's not that at all. I want you to be happy here. You've got all you need. Let's be thankful for what God has given us. Remember there are millions of people around the World who don't have what we have. I just think you need to be careful about her."

"That's the point – she doesn't take what God has given her for granted. That's why she wants to help people – people less fortunate than herself. She doesn't hang around doing nothing. She doesn't bury her talents in the ground. She uses them." He is getting animated.

As always it is during these types of conversation in which the future appears to become clarified. As he argues with his mother he begins to sense God's plan for him. Then he sees it clearly within his mind's eye; together with the evangelist, he is going to save the souls of those less fortunate than themselves. He knows his mother does not understand the true nature of the evangelist or his relationship with her, and she never will - for his mother has never heard the call from God like he is hearing it now. It is the clarion call for action.

They consummated their relationship one weekend at festival of praise to Big Daddy. They went to all the worship gatherings; singing, praying and dancing before returning to the hotel he had paid for them to stay in.

He had booked separate rooms and was somewhat surprised when later that night she entered his room, slipped of her dress, and slid into bed next to him.

The following morning they could both be seen at the breakfast table laughing, crying, and making plans for their future. The victim told the evangelist Big Daddy wanted them to be together and save souls. The evangelist confirmed this as the truth and clarified that the souls they were to save resided in South America - more specifically, in Rio de Janeiro. They had the money to get there – the victim's savings. They could rent a hut on the beach and immerse themselves in the life of the people there. The evangelist explained he had nothing to worry about - this was what Big Daddy had obviously wanted to happen and hadn't Big Daddy made that abundantly clear in all the messages she had been instructed to give him.

They make their plans in secret, booking flights, arranging short term accommodation for when they arrive. And then, approximately one month after the consummation of their relationship, the mother awakes one morning to find her son has left home with a single suitcase and the evangelist in tow, to save lost souls in South America. The victim was convinced, the evangelist was convincing – theirs was the relationship made in heaven blessed to last for eternity.

The victim returned to his mother three months later. He arrived in the town minus a job, his savings, and the evangelist; but with the addition of a newly acquired drug habit and substantial debt. He was never quite able to explain just exactly what had happened.

At the same time the evangelist felt it was probably not appropriate to make an appearance and sensibly decided to remove herself as far away as possible from the part of the country in which the victim lived. She will return to the town in the future for she knows it won't be long before people forget any transgression on her part, especially as she will have had the opportunity to be saved again. She decides it is time to go and see her father – Big Daddy has plans for her future and she now knows exactly what it is.

She is sitting in the warm evening sun, under the arbour, looking out over the lawn and up into the distant hills. She is dressed very demurely in a long white linen dress. She is sitting with her father. There is an ice bucket cooling a bottle of white wine produced from vines grown in the south of country, from a vineyard quite close to the town where she had previously been staying. Her father has dressed for dinner and is wearing a light linen suit over a pink designer silk summer shirt.

"So - did you have a good time in South America?" he asks.

"Yes," she replies, "it gave me much needed space to think out my life."

"What about the boy you were out there with, are you still seeing him?"

"Oh you know – it just didn't work out – mummy's boy and all that – he's gone home to her."

They are silent for a while, each taking a sip of wine from the cut crystal wine glasses. The evangelist sighs dramatically and turns her head upwards to the sun to feel the full effect of the evening heat on her face.

"Daddy, I've been thinking it's about time I made use of the trust fund set up for my education."

The father is agitated. This is the type of conversation which ruins his evening. Every time the evangelist tries to free up the funds held for her in trust with some hare brained plan, it has always ended in heated arguments, tantrums and tears.

"We've been through this before. The trust fund is for your full time education and I will not sanction transferring it to you until you can prove you are in full time education and intend to finish a course which holds some prospect of a career for you. You can't spend the whole of your life floating from one place to another without a care in the World."

"Well that's the point," she replies, "it's taken me a long time to realise what I care about most. You know I have loved God all my life – you brought me up as a good christian – well I have decided to dedicate myself fully to God. I want to go to theological college and become a minister of religion."

She frames her intention very carefully, for her father, as a 'serious 'and devout fundamentalist, does not appreciate her evangelical ecstatic approach to faith. He considers her peculiar brand of religion cheapens the glory of the God he has worshipped reverently since a child. He remains silent for a moment.

"It's not that easy to just turn up at a theological college and expect to be accepted. Do you actually know anyone from any denomination who will support your application?"

The evangelist turns her head up to the sky, silently thanks Big Daddy, turns and looks her father in the eyes.

"Oh yes – I know plenty of people who will support my application."

# Chapter 5 – The Curator

*For the preservation of quality depends on the keeper*
*Yet who understands the nature of the keeping?*

He has never considered himself as lonely, or of his life as being solitary - he is what he is and that should be enough. He wears his heart on his sleeve - he tells it as it is. People have to accept him - accept him for his looks, his opinions, his knowledge, his intellect, and the personal awareness he brings to the World. For he knows, without the shadow of a doubt, it is a better place because he is in it. In fact the World would not exist in the absence of his own existence. The curator is sure of himself and his position in society - though what that position is could be subject to a certain degree of conjecture by even the most average of observers.

He follows a daily routine which he basically adheres to regardless of season or year. His alarm will go off at 6.31 am (he likes the quirkiness of the extra minute in bed) – he will get up, go downstairs to make an instant coffee, then return up the stairs to his office. Once there he will settle himself down in front of his lap top computer to review the news headlines. After he has tutted and grunted his way through the daily digest he will do his toilet, have a shower, shave, brush his hair, clean his teeth, dress, and finally, open up the shrine.

It was his destiny to become the curator and de facto guardian of the shrine. The house belonged to his mother and when she died ten years ago, he, at the grand age of thirty years, being the sole descendent, inherited the whole pile. He has maintained the shrine ever since for the honour and maintenance of her eternal memory. His mother, as he has come to recognise over the years, was a true representation of the Divine Female. It had taken her over twenty years to assemble the shrine after she divorced the father, and the curator is more than happy to spend the rest of his life maintaining it.

The shrine in itself is a rare entity and only the curator knows of its existence, and where it is situated. From the outside it just looks like any other semi-detached house in the leafy suburbs of the over populated city. It has a neat front garden and the mandatory black and green wheelie bins sitting at the near side of the front door. The wooden front entrance to the shrine is painted in a nondescript pale green gloss and is secured with a basic cylinder night latch. It is the perfect disguise for the shrine and nobody would remotely suspect what was hidden and secured within its sacred walls.

The inner sanctum of shrine is housed within what others would call the front living room/lounge. Whilst it is most obviously dedicated to the memory of his eternal mother, over the last ten years, through his own personal management, the space has started to express some of his own unique character and tastes. He has had to make some additions and alterations following her death. This mainly consists of memorabilia which had previously existed quite happily in other parts of the shrine, but as they were personal to the mother, and he needed to requisition the space they occupied for his own administrative purposes, he decided she would appreciate all her belongings residing together in this one room. Consequently the contents within the inner sanctum now reflect, to a certain degree, his own personal conception as to who and what the mother represents.

The shrine underpins and buttresses the personal self-image of who and what he believes himself to be. Obviously he had been shocked by the sudden and unexpected death of the mother and at first he was intimidated by the responsibility of maintaining this sacred place. However as the years have gone by he feels more and more at home with his role.

Every morning as he enters through the hallowed doors, the bizarre collection of colourful objects greet his eyes and vie for the special attention and personal validation which only he can give them. Each item on display brings back a memory of the unique persona that constituted the mother. Every morning he will worshipfully move a piece, and rearrange its position within the overall display initially created by the mother, and finally completed by himself. Each movement, each position adjusted, is made in a ritual of remembrance to the Divine Goddess and is an action bringing him closer to his own personal god – himself.

After a period of prayer and quiet meditation in the inner sanctum he will walk upstairs to his office. His office is now situated in what was once his own personal bedroom. Ten years ago he moved into his mother's boudoir and ever since then has slept in her Queen sized bed. He has also placed his clothes in her double glass mirror fronted wardrobe. It was a source of great pleasure to her, when shortly before her death, she had the wardrobe installed. He knows she would be pleased he is using it for its intended purpose. Every morning, before he goes downstairs to prepare his instant coffee, he will stand naked in front of the mirror admiring his own physique whilst, at the same time, bringing to mind his most glorious and sensuous mother.

Once he has arrived in the office he will sit down and glance at the gold gilt picture frame containing his one treasured photograph of the dear departed mother. He will again bless her memory, log onto to his lap top computer and start typing away on the keyboard.

The curator likes to imagine himself as a bit of a writer, philosopher and scholar. However, his ability to write is questionable and nothing that has left his 'pen 'has been published 'officially'. This does not matter overmuch as he has no need to do anything so mundane as make a living. When his mother passed away she not only left him the house but also a substantial pension fund from which he draws down a monthly 'salary'. His monthly income, when added up over the year, exceeds the average national household income. Nevertheless, regardless of the simple convenience of having more than enough money to cater for his various needs, he does feel obliged to have some sort of profession to identify with, this is in order to provide him with a modicum of credibility when he engages with other human beings.

It is within the peculiar nature of society that everyone appears to be defined by their occupation. Indeed one of the initial questions a person chooses to ask another on first meeting them is something to the effect of," so what is it that you do?" Every application form you are required to complete for this, that, and the other, will generally ask for 'your occupation'. The curator knows instinctively that in order not to draw too much attention to himself, and to make his way through the world with as little hassle as possible, he needs to have some sort of professional occupation. After a great deal of thought he decides to be a writer. In his mind it sounds infinitely more distinguished than having to confess to the tiresome reality he is actually surviving, financially at least, on his deceased mother's pension.

Having chosen to be a writer he decides to take his occupation somewhat seriously. Therefore he has to determine what type of writer he should be. Having reasonably calculated that he did not have the patience or inclination to research and write a novel, he decides to write philosophical tracts shaped from his personal experience, beliefs and values. In his opinion he is well read and has an understanding of the world that very few others, and certainly not those few people he meets on a daily basis, have.

He shares his musings with the World by 'publishing' them online to his personal website alongside a daily blog – which is essentially a rant about everything and anything which has upset him on the news that morning. He is sure one day someone will read his work; his brilliance will be recognised and he will receive the adoration he so clearly deserves. Up until very recently no-one had posted any comment about his work. However, three days ago he received an email from a woman who appeared to be very taken with his writings.

He remains in the office for a few hours busying himself with the important aspects of his life before settling down to relax whilst playing various forms of solitaire on his computer. He proceeds in this solitary way for a few hours, just once stopping in between games to go down stairs and brew a cup of tea. As the inevitable boredom kicks in he looks at his watch and notices with a degree of relief that it is nearly midday.

In order to keep himself engaged in the 'real 'world, everyday, at precisely midday, he takes his lunch break in the pub just down the road from where he lives. He arrives at the Four Feathers, an early twentieth century public house owned by the local city brewery, just as the local church bells chime the hour.

The Four Feathers is a non-entity pub, one of the varieties which always look as if it was last renovated around twenty years previously. Consequently you will notice nicotine stains on the once white ceiling and cigarette burns on the once colourful striped orange carpet. It is a tired pub, run by a tired landlady for a tired clientele who meet there every lunch with such regularity that should one of them not to turn up they would ring around to see whether the person had fallen ill, had been taken to hospital, or died in his sleep.

It is in this pub where the curator will spend a two hour 'lunch break ' chewing the cud with his fellow regulars whilst scanning the newspaper. His fellow regulars - there are five in total - are of an age unverifiable because of the amount of alcohol they have ingested every lunchtime since retirement.

The regulars find the curator mildly amusing and have privileged him with the honorific title of 'Young Un'. They will always ask the 'Young Un 'for an opinion on whatever national or local issue has raised its fussy presence into the fore-front of their equally fuzzy thinking. Whatever the subject the curator will have a view, even if he has no direct experience and knows absolutely nothing about the matter under discussion. As a writer he prides himself of being able to put himself within the shoes of other people and imagine how they think and feel.

It is probably a shame that he does not apply this trait when communicating in person with his fellow human beings. The curator is proud of the life he leads and is convinced that sharing his experience and personal philosophy for living can only be of help to his listeners. If they are not responsive to his message he does not worry for it is obvious the recipient of his discourse has neither the wit nor intelligence to understand the depth of his meaning or recognise the elemental importance of the truth he is revealing.

The lunch time clientele at the Four Feathers generate a somewhat masculine atmosphere. The curator finds the scent of aged misogynistic testosterone particular suited to the mentality of his lunchtime lectures as the majority of his personal philosophy, of which he has much to share, is about Women and the worship of the female. As a writer the curator knows it is vital to test out his ideas and theories with an audience – it helps develop his writing; enabling his scribblings to flesh out and take on a more revealing form.

Several years ago he realised the tenor of his vocabulary was making it difficult for the average layman to understand the core of what he was trying to convey. Consequently he has developed a linguistic style which specialises in four and five letter words. These he uses prolifically with great aplomb to shock the listener into deeper levels of thinking. He knows this is a tried and tested teaching method used by the some of the very greatest philosophers from antiquity. Therefore he considers this direct form is an appropriate mode of communication in all situations. An introductory question he finds particularly effective and which he uses frequently on unsuspecting male listeners is, "How is pussy? Are you getting enough?" Generally the shock this question engenders places the curator in a position of power over the often reluctant listener for the duration of their ongoing dialogue.

At exactly two pm he will return to the shrine, enter the front door, remove his shoes and place them on a rack next to the door, put on his house shoes, climb up the stairs, enter his office, open his diary, and make copious notes relating to the personal observations he has made along with the resulting revelations which have occurred to him as a product of his lunchtime soiree. He will stay in the office for around an hour at which point he will suddenly decide to have another cup of tea. He then climbs down the stairs, walks across the hallway and into the small galley which houses the kitchen. He pours water from the hot tap into a kettle, switches the kettle on to boil the water, places a teabag into a large chipped purple mug, and takes a bottle of full cream milk out of the fridge. After the water has boiled he will combine all the ingredients together to create what he humorously likes to consider as being 'builders 'strength tea'.

Clutching the mug containing the murky brown liquid, he will walk down the hall and open the door to the inner sanctum. There he will sit in quiet reflection allowing the steam from the mug to create a film of perspiration on his face. After an hour the mug will have been emptied of its contents and he will then return to the kitchen to start the preparation of his evening meal. Whilst he flexes his culinary skills he will be aided and abetted by the accompaniment of the radio.

At six pm he enters the dining room, pushing the door open with his foot whilst clutching a tray containing his food in one hand and the half empty bottle of red wine he has just removed from the fridge, held tightly in the other. He will sit quietly at the table, for there is no-one else there to talk to, eat his food, drink a glass of wine, and complete the daily crossword. At seven thirty pm he will, after washing up the dirty dishes and placing the remaining red wine back in fridge, retrace his footsteps up the stairs and into his mother's boudoir. He will undress and slip in to the queen sized bed, lie on his back, stare at the ceiling, sigh with relief at being able to complete another day successfully, and, fall asleep.

For the last ten years since the death of his mother the curator has fixed his attention on one subject alone. During this period it is the only topic he has written on in any depth. It is an ongoing philosophical reasoning on the sexuality of Woman. He has undertaken this project in memory of, and in honour to, his mother.

Everything he knows about women and femininity he learnt from his mother – and it has to be said she was a very good teacher. The latest tract in his ongoing series of papers is entitled ' –In Glorification of the

Sexuality in the Divine Woman'. It has been twelve months in formation and in its final genesis consists of exactly 2,362 words. The central tenet of the thesis relates to the God given nature of the all encompassing cradle of life which lies between the thighs of the female of the species, and how this cradle should be glorified by the penetration of the member that resides in a similar area on the male of the species. It is this particular 'paper', posted on his website and other social media, which has resulted in the first ever response being made in respect to his writing. It was from the woman.

'I am a research fellow at the city university and have just read your posting with a great deal of interest as the subject matter is one I have a certain expertise in. I would like to discuss your writing with you, and maybe share some of our mutual knowledge in this particular and fascinating area of anthropological research. My telephone number is given below – please give me a call.'

He has spent the last three days intermittently reading and re-reading the message. This contact with a larger society existing beyond the confines of the shrine and the Four Feathers public house generates deep feelings of anticipation and excitement marred by equivalent sensations of anxiety and unease. He contemplates meeting the woman in the 'flesh'.

He has never 'been out' with a woman during the whole of his life to date. Naturally, he has spoken to them occasionally especially if he has encountered one in the pub. But he has never had any form of direct personal social engagement with any woman whatsoever other than his mother. He has certainly never met one for coffee. He has no friends or relatives of the female sex. It is something he has thought, considered, and occasionally even fantasised about, however, his life as curator, with its responsibilities towards the mother, has previously prevented him from contemplating ever making the move to find a female friend. He is not a virgin - not by any stretch of the imagination; yet he has never had a girlfriend. So on this particular day he breaks with his rigid routine and makes the sudden and abrupt decision to contact the woman immediately.

At precisely six pm, before he commences his evening meal, he picks up the phone and calls the correspondent. Fortuitously, before he has a chance to feel any guilt towards his dear departed mother, she answers the phone and, after a very brief discussion, arranges to meet the curator the following day in a local coffee shop of her choice.

The coffee shop she chooses is one of the typical chain variety which exist in most city high streets. This one has a small frontage which belies the fact that its main drinking area stretches back over 100 feet. It sits next to a river with three large bi-fold glass doors that provide both a view over the water and access to a patio kitted out with plastic rattan settees surrounded by low level wooden coffee tables. Whilst these have been purchased for allweather use it would seem, from their overall appearance, that the weather has chosen to abuse them for more years than they would care to remember. This abuse, coinciding with the abuse they receive from the smokers who were banished to these seats many years ago, and who have still not managed to develop the manual dexterity to use ash trays for their intended purpose, provide the seating with a sad and rather unhealthy complexion.

He arrives thirty minutes before they are due to meet and sits at a table with a view to the door. He remains there clutching a double shot skinny latte with his heart doing little skips and beats every time a lady comes through the door. During the following half an hour he experiences a great deal of heart jumping as women of every shape and form seem to arrive at this particular coffee shop on this particular day to meet friends at eleven am.

Finally she arrives, six minutes late. If you were to ask him how he knew it was her he wouldn't know. They certainly had not prearranged any method for identifying the other. Maybe it was the way his heart jumped a little higher – more likely it was because she was six minutes late and the odds were stacking up she would shortly make an entrance, with no friends, prams or family in tow.

She is tall, handsome, with long auburn hair. She is smartly and expensively clothed in soft pastel tunic and trousers, these are surrounded by a long cardigan of raw natural silk which reaches down in a continuous flow of elegance to her ankles. He observes her critically - as one would carefully examine a work of art. He does this surreptitiously in a way that he hopes is not obvious - he wouldn't want to appear rude. Nevertheless, he cannot help but admire what he perceives to be her bountiful breasts and the smoothness of stomach gliding towards her inner thighs. Yes, he thinks, this is what an eternal divine goddess of fertility would look like in the flesh.

For all his excitement their initial introduction and pleasantries appear mundane. She determines the variety of coffee she is going to drink and they agree to sit outside overlooking the river – it is quiet out there and they will not be disturbed by screaming babies in prams – also it will be easier to converse without having to consider any others who may, by accident, start listening in to their deeply philosophical conversation.

"I am so pleased you agreed to meet me," she says.

The formal part of the proceedings has just commenced.

"As I mentioned in my email the subject you are researching; sexuality and gender, is one I have particular interest in and I like meeting people who are interested in the subject and are prepared, as they say, to put their head above the parapet and express their views. I hope you feel ok to talk about the last article you posted."

The Curator can't believe his luck – he is beginning to have the type of social interaction he has missed since his mother's premature death ten years ago. In an instant he can tell that at last he is conversing with someone who is his intellectual equal.

"Of course I am more than happy to share my insights with you," he replies, "as I think you would agree from reading my latest paper, I respect women and glorify in their sexuality. My mother brought me up to recognise the wonder of sex and the beauty of sexual attraction. She taught me the sanctity of sexual intimacy and how one should respect and view the physical act of consummation between man and woman as a sacrament deserving of the most holy reverence."

She looks at him closely. Personally she is surprised by what she sees. He is much better looking than she expected and the sudden attraction she feels towards him confuses her for a moment.

Her particular area of anthropological research currently relates to growing prevalence of misogynistic behaviours through social media. She came across the curator's article as part of a larger trawl on the internet searching for material which would support her initial findings. She rather impetuously posted her message onto his website after reading his ludicrous article and rather foolishly agreed to meet him when he rang in response. As he was local she thought it would be both interesting and amusing to meet him and get a sense of what a misogynist behaved like in the flesh. She pauses and then speaks.

"Then I hope you won't mind me feeding back my initial perceptions of your work. Personally I find your paper to contain nothing more than the misogynistic shite of an underindulged male mind."

She provides her feedback neutrally, with no rancour or criticism even suggested within the tone of her voice. She is smiling at him, but is perfectly serious. To any outsider looking on you would have thought she was talking about the quality of the coffee she was drinking.

However, this wasn't quite what she had been planning to say. She had intended to probe his mind with psychologically inspired questions in an attempt to understand how a human being could possibly reason in the way he obviously does. She laughs inwardly at herself as she now realises she rather fancies the misogynistic idiot. Her emotional response both annoys and intrigues her. She smiles and continues speaking.

"You write with a very low and insipid understanding of feminine sexuality. What I am reading appears to me a product of an adolescent boy having difficulties with his hormones. I know sex and the deepest secrets of female sexuality – I have spent many years researching them across many different cultural traditions. I do not believe you have a clue about what it really means to worship a woman and I am really interested to know if you have ever seriously tried to find out."

The curator listens to the feedback and feels the full force of a personal revelation. He realises he doesn't know his subject well enough – this was why he hasn't yet received the recognition he knows he richly deserves. He looks at the woman and feels the world move within his loins, up through his stomach, through his chest and heart and towards to his head which starts thudding and buzzing with excitement. The waves of energy continues to flow up and down his body for several seconds as he concludes the person opposite him is the woman to be worshipped, adored and sanctified.

Likewise the woman is equally confused. She is smitten by the sudden feelings she has toward the man sitting opposite to her. She is unable to see the misogynist within the body of the rather good looking man sitting opposite - yet he obviously is a misogynist, isn't he? Maybe he has just never met the right woman - or any woman come to that.

She continues observing him, and very slowly, and certainly going against her deeply held personal values and beliefs - recognises a man she would like to have children with.

At least once in every life there is a time when each member of humanity will meet the kindred spirit - a person who will change the path of their life beyond what was ever initially conceived. Possibly the moment is co-ordinated by the 'movement of the spheres' as a part of each individual's unique destiny - the meeting of one's soul partner. Generally, when this momentous occasion arises, each party to the transaction will be confused by both their attraction to each other and how it ever arose. Regardless of any possible denial the recipients of the gift will realise deep down in the pit of their belly that they have found each other, and, whether they like it or not their life has been irrevocably changed for better or for worse. Sometimes, of course, this little gift will be squandered - the chance will not be taken and the moment will pass by with the individuals involved contemplating for the rest of their lives what might have been.

He insists on dinner that very day - then another dinner on a different day - then lunch and a drink at a traditional seventeenth century coaching inn opposite the city cathedral. Eventually, about a fortnight later in the sanctity of her bedroom, she introduces him to the deepest secrets of female sexuality she had alluded to on the very first day they met. He is lost, captivated, and paralysed within the comfort of his total worship and adoration towards her.

As with all relationships there is momentary lull within the daily lust where each participant begins to recognise the sum of their collective parts have momentarily become a singular whole. This perceptual quantum leap is achieved when each individual perceives within the other a person the ability to acknowledge and validate their daily existence. Whilst there is no general rule of thumb as to when this happens, for the curator and the woman it occurs within the first three months following their initial coffee together.

Obviously there are concerns – there always will. The woman has a past and so does the curator. At this early stage in their relationship they are still not feeling secure enough with each other to share all the aspects of their previous incarnations. They have covered the basic facts and discover they do have a great deal in common.

His mother had been wonderful, his father had been unfaithful, his mother divorces father, he never sees his father again.

She also has a wonderful mother who was her father's second wife. The father is a philanderer and the mother catches him in bed with a best friend. Mother divorces father and the daughter chooses never to speak to the father again.

As a result of this shared experience and their obvious compatibility in the bedroom, they trust one another enough to contemplate fulfilling the desire to share a living space. They are both old enough to make this decision; they are also both financially independent. The main difference between the two of them is that he owns a house whilst she rents an apartment in the centre of the city.

It may seem odd, but during these first three months, the curator has never invited the woman to the shrine that is the main place of his residence. Some deep nagging guilt concerning the sanctity of his relationship with the deceased mother has prevented him from doing so. Now he has finally suggested she should probably move in with him to free up the income she has been 'blowing away' on monthly rental payments, utility bills and council tax.

Naturally she is quite intrigued to see the curator's bachelor pad. She hasn't minded entertaining him in her own apartment as she had a feeling it would be more comfortable and hygienic. It had also been more convenient to make him do all the commuting to her rather than her to him. In all honesty, she has no real intention of moving in with him, she is more interested to see what it would fetch financially on the open market. She has decided they need to buy a place they can call their own and design it interiorly in the spirit of their unique personalities.

She is less than happy about the location of his dwelling. She doesn't like the suburb in which the house is situated. The house is far too close to a public house, the Four Feathers, which just happens to be where her estranged father goes every lunchtime for his daily gin and tonic. She hasn't yet shared her plans to purchase a property with the curator for she is well aware he has some peculiar long standing sense of commitment which could prevent him from agreeing to sell the house left to him by his mother. However, she is fairly certain that on close inspection of his home she will find many reasons for not moving in and will subsequently persuade him to place it on the open market.

They park his car on the side of the road next to the semi detached house in the leafy suburbs of the over populated city and within which he has lived all his life. She walks up the front garden path and past the black and green wheelie bins and waits as he unlocks the nondescript pale green gloss front door.

As she enters the hallway she is astonished at how bright, airy and clean the house feels. It does not give the impression of being a man's house at all; she can definitely feel the touch of a woman in the whole way the property is organised. She is quite pleasantly surprised; the garden is neat and tidy revealing a degree of taste and a horticultural ability she was, quite frankly, not expecting. As she looks around the rest of the house it appears functional and she is beginning to consider that it may just be worth giving up her apartment and living here whilst they sell the property and commence the search to find somewhere more suitable for sharing their life together.

She finds the office endearing, especially when he explains the old poster, showing the Jesus of Scandinavian alliteration with blonde beard and piercing bright blue eyes, has been living on the wall, in exactly the same place since his earliest childhood memories. This had been his bedroom and he explains he had copied and coloured the rather childish looking drawing of a plant, that acts as a frame for the poster, from the one which had been embroidered onto the bedroom curtains.

As they continue the tour of the upstairs portion of the house she discovers that the bathroom, shower and toilet are surprisingly clean. She feels the main bedroom is little kitsch and outdated. Nevertheless it would be fine once they moved her king size bed in, start using her fine Egyptian cotton linen, and replaced the curtains. The other bedroom is functional although slightly small. The only room she has left to explore is the main living room downstairs. For some reason the curator has left this room out of the itinerary so far.

The curator is very nervous about allowing the woman entry into the inner sanctum of the shrine. However, at this stage in the proceedings it can no longer be avoided, and anyway he is feeling slightly more comfortable after registering the occasional murmurs of approval which escapes from the lips of the woman as she inspects the overall fabric of the estate she is being asked to live in.

They walk down the stairs to the glass door beyond the side door of the dining room. He mumbles something about how this was his mother's room, her pride and joy. She opens the door.

As she stands at the door she is transported back twenty years. The walls of the room have been sponge painted in pastel green. A grapevine ripe with purple fruits dripping from its branches has been stencilled all around the top of the walls and around the windows. Floral patterned curtains hang at each side fastened to brass fittings. A five light candelabra with bulbs shrouded in leaf shaped shades hangs from the centre of the ceiling. There is a large corner settee, over stuffed and covered in a light beige fabric and decorated with cushions covered with celestial patterns of blue and yellow. Opposite the settee there is a Versailles gold leaf shabby chic gilt chaise longue. On the glass coffee table in between them there is an arrangement of fake silk flowers and a couple of old vogue magazines. Taking the focal point of the room there is a first generation widescreen silver grey analogue television with integral video player/recorder. Hanging from the wall, to the left and right hand side of the fireplace, are dresses, blouses, braziers, tights and all manner of apparel which must have belonged to the mother. On top the mantelpiece of, positioned as if on a church altar, are four old vodka bottles with candles placed into the neck stem. The room smells of lavender. She looks at the curator.

"I never got around to taking the clothes to the charity shop and they just somehow got left in here?" he voice is sounding distinctly nervous.

She ignores him for the moment and stares at the pyjamas and purple house coat which appear to be placed in position of honour at each side of the fireplace.

She looks around the room, it has a lived in quality about it. It is obvious it is cleaned regularly. There is the shocking realisation as everything starts to make sense. All of those tiny inconsistencies she had been concerned about but had not really questioned, join up to reveal a new insight into the person she is standing next to. Her heart starts to beat slightly quicker. She takes a deep breathe and turns towards the curator.

"If you expect me to move into this house absolutely everything goes and it will have to be redecorated from top to bottom." She speaks with the same neutral toned voice he first experienced in the coffee shop and which he has now learnt hides the emotional edge that should never be questioned.

He stares back at her and then lowers his eyes away from her steady gaze. He is beginning to feel a deep sense of anxiety tying an extremely tight knot in the region of his bowels.

"I can't do that. This is mother's own creation. She spent hours creating the room for us both to share. She did it after my father left us. It was only me and her from then on. She taught me everything about the intimate nature of femininity and what it means to be a woman. When she was dying I promised to look after the house for her. Keep it clean in respect for the life she gave me." He sounds desperate as he starts to realise that a way of being himself could well be coming to an abrupt end.

She looks at him and contemplates his confusion. She realises they have arrived at a point of no return. They will either stay together or she will walk out now. She makes her decision very quickly. In the silence which follows she slowly takes his hand and places inside the top of her trouser and starts moving it slowly downwards. She places her other hand on the crotch of his trousers and starts moving it up and down. He groans with pleasure.

"Well my darling, do you want pussy or your mummy?"

He searches his mind for an answer fitting for the occasion. Then with the reflection of an emotion that comes with the recollection of everything that has ever transpired in the shrine, he turns to the woman and replies quite simply –

"You know, I think I would like them both."

She maintains eye contact, smiles at him, and replies in the calm voice of a mother addressing a wayward child. It is a voice which requires total and utter obedience.

"Well my sweet, I think you will have to choose me for I have plans for you, and do you know what - your mummy's dead."

# Chapter 6 – The Bright Young Things

'A life not photographed
Is a life not lived.'

They meet on a mid-morning chat show - one which is aired each weekday on national television - chaperoned under the watchful eye of the host, who can immediately sense the embryonic sparks of young love shooting through the atmosphere of the small television theatre like the spores of a fungus seeking a new home in which to germinate and grow. The bright young things - both adepts in the art of inner self-contentment - often appear as guests on such day time shows to divulge how you, the viewer, can become as self-contented as they are. Today is the first time their paths have crossed professionally, and, discerning within the other a like-minded soul eager for self-publicity, immediately recognise the potential to join forces and reveal the path that has led each of them to their current state of unmitigated bliss and spiritual awareness, to an unsuspecting yet equally market ready audience.

The bright young things share a resolute desire and rapacious need for personal recognition, not just from their nearest and dearest, but from the rest of the World. They want the adoration and the grateful acknowledgement of all who see them in the street. They crave celebrity.

Of course true celebrity status is quite difficult to attain and once attained even harder to maintain, especially through the standard routes of music, art, literature, politics, drama and sport - these paths are not only extremely competitive in nature and also require a degree of effort, especially in terms of application and dedication. Whilst they had both been immensely popular amongst their peers at school and subsequent universities, neither of them displayed any particular talent or inclination towards these honourable and cherished pursuits. However, they did possess an unnerving ability towards self-publicity and promotion.

For a couple of years after leaving university each of them were unsure of the career path they should follow except that whatever it was should ultimately lead them to fame and fortune. She left university with a 2:2 in theatre studies and he attained a 2:2 in social history. Both sets of parents where relatively wealthy, so they decided, individually of course, to travel and explore the world at their progenitors' expense - they needed the time to reflect on their futures.

It was during their independent travels around India they both hit upon the idea of becoming psycho-spiritual gurus. They had both dabbled in meditation, a bit of yoga, and developed a taste for those new age self help courses which enabled participants to wallow in the joy of being themselves. What they also both noticed was how the workshop leaders, whilst enabling participants to recognise and acknowledge their own self-importance, encouraged total devotion and love towards themselves. Surely this was a career that ticked all the boxes - a career that would lead to celebrity, a career in which they would be loved, admired, and adored. Over the following couple of years they developed the individual key elements of what, when they finally met, would become known as 'The Religion of Least Effort (RLE™)'.

'The Religion of Least Effort (RLE™) 'is an assemblage of all those nice cuddly bits of loving dogma often found and celebrated within most of the world's main religions. These are then blended with a little serving of astrology, numerology and pop psychology with a seasoning of guided meditation thrown in for good measure. Anything that is remotely complicated and difficult to comprehend or put into practice is left outside its broad church. So, for example, the rather complex doctrine of universal forgiveness, as expounded in a number of spiritual traditions, is restricted to a somewhat superficial variant enabling the forgiveness of self. It works very simply - if you realise that you have committed a sin against someone else, and, although feeling slightly ashamed and embarrassed about your behaviour you can't face the inconvenience of having to accept fault in person - write down your transgression on a piece of paper and burn it ceremoniously whilst incanting the words - 'I forgive myself and you forgive me'. Then feel free to carry on your life as if nothing has ever happened.

Likewise, if you believe someone else has done you wrong – don't waste your time exploring the issue with them – drop them out of your life immediately - they are no longer relevant in your search for perfected inner self-contentment. The ceremony involves the writing of a letter - a personal one addressed to your transgressor setting out the grievance and the pain they have caused you. You should then burn it ceremoniously whilst incanting the words  - 'your transgressions will not harm me as you have no relevance in my life'. The smoke arising from the flames will travel through the aether and advise them of your decision to exclude them from your person, thus ensuring you will never have to confront your once upon a time friend ever again, or suffer the inconvenience of having a difficult conversation with them.

In the 'The Religion of Least Effort (RLE™) 'confrontation with another person is to be avoided at all costs. Any form of personal conflict is frowned upon as it reduces the ability to love yourself and to flaunt that love in front of others.

Shortly after their TV appearance they decide to pool resources. Within a couple of months they announce their marriage in Florida in a private ceremony attended by family and friends. They return to the country, move into a large house in countryside, and celebrate the event by buying, as a lasting memorial to the consummation of their nuptials, a brand new cream Mercedes motor vehicle with black leather seats and mahogany wood trimmings.

In outward appearance the bright young things are what most people would define as perfect in every way. She is a natural blonde with blue eyes and hour glass figure - he is tall, dark, slim and handsome with deep grey eyes. They dress in the most fashionable of designer clothes and from the outside appear to live the most perfect of lives.

In her dreams of celebrity she had imagined for herself the most perfect of marriages. From childhood she had created an exquisite world where she was loved and adored by all around her. And obviously, from her point of view, it was her new husband's destiny to help her achieve all she had ever dreamed of. Likewise he had always dreamt of the perfect wife - beautiful and intelligent and willing to sacrifice all to support him in the fulfilment of his destiny. Whether, prior to the marriage, they were aware of this, they certainly became cognisant to it shortly afterwards - and, to be honest, both were content to play out each other's fantasy. There was a certain style to be attained and maintained - the Mercedes was only the start.

On their return from Florida they set about the joint creation of 'The Religion of Least Effort (RLE™)'. It becomes their obsession. Their whole life is dedicated to its creation. Before long they have conceived a methodology which is neatly packaged, commoditised, marketed and sold to a population obviously in need of their spiritual expertise. The conceptualisation supporting this new religion, and the products required to promulgate its practise, slowly gain recognition within the UK, then in America, then in Europe, and finally in India.

What they individually contribute to' The Religion of Least Effort (RLE™) 'is subtly different in form and content – she nurtures a creative loving feminine form to the religion, whilst he develops a more, and in his own opinion, practical and masculine approach. The former can be described as pseudo mystical and the latter as pseudo psychological. However there is a clear definable link between the two which has given their creation the appearance of being a unified and indivisible whole.

Naturally they are the recognised and un-challenged spiritual leaders of 'The Religion of Least Effort (RLE™)' - quite simply the whole edifice is created in the golden reflection of their own enlightenment. They don't feel the need to formally determine what their roles and responsibilities are in relation to each other - they are god and goddess. They hold no formal meetings and nothing agreed between them, other than their marriage, is set down in any kind of legally binding contract – for to create legal agreements and establish formalised operational protocols raises the possibility for the need to have difficult conversations and, as mentioned previously, such emotionally challenging interactions go against the fundamental precepts of 'The Religion of Least Effort (RLE™)'.

As a result the administrative functions that evolve out of organic need, financial necessity and legal impositions are generally left to their accountants and solicitors to deal with. They have no wish to be involved with the mundanity of such processes. They obviously require a certain amount of money in order to maintain their chosen lifestyle as spiritual celebrities, and this desideratum grows on a yearly basis. Transcendental enlightenment cannot be offered to the general proletariat on a no fee basis – gurus, such as themselves, and like all those others who came before them, have physical and emotional needs which require gratification. They deserve to be remunerated at whatever rate the market can support. This is only just and is in recognition for all the hard labour they undertake, and to recompense them for the personal sacrifices they have made on behalf of society.

Indeed there is a large market of economically viable individuals suitably dissatisfied and disappointed with what life has thrown at them. They are willing to be saved and pay handsomely for the privilege and constantly spend their life searching for the next new spiritual fad which may temper the loneliness of their egos. Consequently, there will always be a demand within the self-help, spoil and pamper yourself marketplace for any new pseudo-spiritual psychological path offering peace and enlightenment for the needy narcissist and workshop junkie. With its promise of helping adherents to develop unparalleled levels of inner self-contentment 'The Religion of Least Effort (RLE™) 'offers a pleasant, un-challenging, albeit expensive pastime dispensing much needed balm to the wounds sustained in their damaged experience of life.

The bright young things mine this market mercilessly – for they know that while they increase their own personal wealth and wellbeing, they are helping their fellow human beings by selling them a product they truly need. Nevertheless within a few years it becomes apparent that if they wish to attain the global recognition they desire, the business will need to grow at a substantially faster rate than the current demand for their services allow. To maximise market potential they need to attract a larger number of clients who are prepared to live life in accordance with the precepts of their thinking.

They therefore decide to establish the professional certificated training, qualifying their more ardent supporters to become fully licensed Adept Teachers in the 'The Religion of Least Effort (RLE™) 'method of inner self-contentment. She adopts the role as international director of learning, responsible for designing the programme and the training of Adepts, while he assumes the marketing and public relations role as a charismatic prophet roaming the World giving lectures to large audiences of people who are seeking the secrets of inner self-contentment. It is a win/win situation for both of them, existing and trainee Adepts are always prepared to attend his lectures and assist him, whilst delegates, more often than not hypnotised by the whole show, end up wanting to undertake the three year training which will result in them becoming qualified Adept Teachers in the art of inner self-contentment.

As the years trickle by, they become increasingly concerned over the financial and marketing ramifications concerning the promotion of their own unique personal and individual brands, together with the need to protect them. Whilst they would both deny 'The Religion of Least Effort (RLE™) 'is a cult of personality, they consider that in all reality its continuing welfare and ongoing development relies primarily upon their own physical graft. It is apparent the organisation is not independently strong enough to exist without their guidance, nurturing care, and complete control over the way it is practised. Therefore, as 'The Religion of Least Effort (RLE™)'s ongoing existence depends on them personally, they recognise an increasing need for being seen in public promoting the appropriate image that reveals to the masses the extraordinary levels of spiritual enlightenment they have both attained.

In order to achieve this perfectly reasonable goal, they begin to develop friendships with other similarly upwardly mobile spiritual gurus who also happen to be operating with some financial success within the 'self help, spoil and pamper yourself' marketplace. After a little consideration these individuals and couples prove to be more than happy to oblige the bright young things with their casual acquaintanceship, recognising the power that the publicity of personal patronage has on generally improving their own financial bottom line.

Within a very short space of time the ad-hoc society for mutual aggrandisement is established. Being a member of this privileged collective leads to guest appearances at each and everyone's training programmes. There will also be the invitations to social engagements, generally group dinners in celebrated local restaurants where, overhearing their rather loud conversations, lesser members of the human race can can sit, admire and reflect on their collective brilliance and spiritual enlightenment. Naturally within such rarefied company there is much to be discussed and debated. The wonderful anecdotes which stem from their soirees are too beautiful not to be shared with the rest of the world and will be used as 'fill in' material on their ongoing lecture, training and seminar schedules, revealing just how wonderful their select friendships are - developed and nurtured on a purely philanthropic basis for your benefit.

Whilst the whole rationale of their existence is in saving the ordinary lesser mortal, they feel it is potentially damaging to their personal brand and self-image to be seen outside the confines of their work engaging or consorting with them – they are both instinctively aware this 'breaks boundaries 'and reduces the mystique of the spiritual authority they are endeavouring to create. Consequently they have established strict rules of engagement. They will never engage with a lesser ordinary mortal outside of their public working environment and even within such settings communication will be limited to those of a non-personal nature.

Likewise they agree the lesser ordinary mortals should never ever be encouraged to commune with them whilst they are consorting with their very select friends. They manage to do this by ensuring there will never be any social event where these two distinctly different social classes could accidentally meet on a 'level playing field'. So for key celebratory occasions, where it would reasonably be expected for them to hold parties, for example Christmas and birthdays, they will organise two separate gatherings to ensure no-one is duly embarrassed by having to associate and engage with people outside their zone of personal comfort. One gathering, generally rather glitzy and expensive, will be for their important celebrity acquaintances, the details of which will be promoted heavily in order to generate some positive publicity within those magazines which matter to them. The other will be for those acquaintances of lesser importance, but who, nevertheless, the bright young things feel the need to acknowledge and thank for some form of service to them. Naturally these functions will receive no publicity whatsoever. They see this as the only right and proper way in which to preserve and respect the dignity and privacy of all concerned.

The years continue to trickle by and they are blissfully enveloped in the market of their making. The bright young things are financially successful, independent and secure. They have the one child, who has been placed out of sight and mind at The Boarding School, their own alma mater. They have become celebrities in the peculiar bubble that is the wider mind, body, and spirit community, and therefore don't need to worry too excessively about the scrutiny or the intrusion of the daily tabloids. Quite simply they operate within a select field which news editors and their readership are not particularly interested in – unless, of course, you happen to be one of those unfortunate guru's discovered practicing some form of sexual deviance not recognised as acceptable or advisable within your own religious discipline.

This state of affairs suits them well, for whilst there are no articles about them in the cheap glossy weekly gossip magazines catering for the uninterested and unenlightened, there are plenty of articles about them in the expensive magazines which cater for and supply much needed sustenance to their own curious market place. They are regular contributors to several of these publications, in which he proffers brotherly advice of a psychological nature to his fellow men, whilst she has become the spiritual agony aunt to her sisters, advising on all issues from spiritual child birth, the spiritual development of the young, sexual liberation in freedom spirituality, the spiritual marriage, and, how to love yourself spiritually.

All the interactions with their followers, be it lectures, training seminars or workshop, are recorded and marketed for sale. These 'products 'cater for the ever increasing demand for their own particular brand of spirituality. Their books on inner self-contentment and the practice of 'The Religion of Least Effort (RLE™) 'sell all over the world and they now hold an international conference once a year to promote and celebrate the 'The Religion of Least Effort (RLE™)'.

The four day annual conference is a family affair for the adherents of 'The Religion of Least Effort (RLE™)'and generally attracts over two thousand delegates, who come and stay in the large country house hotel hired for the duration of the event. Whilst they are there, delegates will attend speeches by him, rituals by her, meditations by both, and a variety of workshops run by either one of them. In the main conference room the daily speeches are filmed and streamed on-line so that anyone who cannot attend does not feel left out of the joyous celebrations.

The stage set up is both beautiful and commanding. There are shrines housing the variety of deities and prophets which the 'The Religion of Least Effort (RLE™) 'have decided to call their own. So Shiva , Krishna, and Ganesh, provide sanctuary along with Jesus, Muhammad, a variety of buddhas, and a visual representation of the Shekinha. The stage is decked out front to back with floral arrangements of white flowers – mostly lilies. For the backdrop to the stage there are two twenty foot portraits of the bright young things looking peaceful, serene, and full of inner self-contentment. If you look at the portraits closely you will notice an aura has been captured floating above their heads that closely resembles the halo often seen in medieval representations of saints. In between the portraits is the symbol 'The Religion of Least Effort (RLE™) 'has adopted as its own. It is a sign made up of an ornate black cross set on a golden six pointed star surrounded with a silver circle.

Although still not expressly laid down in any form of legal or procedural documentation, the roles and responsibilities adopted by the bright young things for the efficient operation of their business have now, by default, become completely defined, delineated, and operate relatively smoothly. They each have their individual tasks which they undertake diligently for the sake of their business and their own continuing self aggrandisement. Nevertheless, whilst they constantly proclaim their uttermost trust in, and undying love for one another, they still choose to exercise a degree of oversight into what their other half is doing – carefully monitoring that he, or she, is individually nurturing, through diligent practice, the very ethos of their religion. Naturally, if asked, they would deny any underlying insecurity in their relationship, sensing that over the years the link which binds them and their business together is becoming stronger, increasingly permanent and un-breakable - for they are, according to their own oft repeated mantra, soul brother, soul sister, and soul lovers.

Their life continues to the insistent beat of a heavy schedule required to maintain their desired levels of success and personal recognition. They are constantly working on this and that and have even had to make a rule they will spend at least one day a week in their marital home together – for if she's not running workshops at a weekend, he will be away running a conference somewhere else. The Weekly Dinner is their special treat - a delightfully delicious three course meal which they will prepare together. They will dress up, light the candles, and open a bottle of their favourite French white wine which they buy directly and collect by the case from the vineyard of some special friends in the Bourgogne. They will sit and talk at the table for three to four hours before finally deciding it is time for bed.

Over the years they each acquire their own inner circle of disciples – people they depend upon to fulfil the routine administrative and secretarial duties required for the effective operation of their personal work schedules. These disciples adore and venerate the guru they work for and have personally avowed their total and utter commitment to their welfare. Whilst all the disciples are followers of 'The Religion of Least Effort (RLE™)', the two distinct groupings are extremely particular in their loyalty to whichever one of the spouses they serve and rarely meet together except at the annual conferences. When they do congregate together it is immediately apparent to the outside observer that underneath the facade of deep respect, fraternal and sororal love, there is, in fact, a deeper level of reserve, jealousy and suspicion. Each group of disciples honour and love their own particular guru beyond measure - they want whatever is best for either her or him, without necessarily caring too much about the impact of their behaviour on the other.

The inevitable game of 'mine is bigger than yours 'develops so slowly it would take the most astute observer of human behaviour to perceive it occurring in real time. As the old saying implies, hindsight is an inept tool for dealing with an issue whilst it is materialising in the future present. Anyway all major religions and spiritual doctrines inevitably suffer from a schism of one sort or another and 'The Religion of Least Effort (RLE™) 'was not going to be an exception to that rule.

It happened gradually, as it always does. One group of disciples start to make seemingly innocuous comments to their preferred guru about the other along the lines of;' wouldn't we be able to do our job more creatively if we had a little less input from........ 'To begin with the bright young things are open about what is being said to them in private and enjoy discussing the antics of their various disciples over the Weekly Dinner – it amuses them. They laugh off the 'innocuous 'comments over their glass of wine deciding the disciples' views and remarks should never ever be taken seriously. Naturally, within their discussions they are particularly careful to follow the precepts of 'The Religion of Least Effort (RLE™) 'and avoid discussing any matter that may impinge on their individual levels of inner self-contentment.

Nevertheless, over a short period of time, they each begin to feel a slight degree of unease about the other's disciples and they both begin to observe and view the actions of the other's group of followers with, what can only be described as, suspicion. They question and scrutinise the motives of each individual disciple, especially if the disciple is of the opposite sex to the guru they are serving. Of course this is done politely and discretely over the dinner table whilst avoiding the need to have any difficult conversation. Neither of them really believe that they, themselves personally, are going to succumb to the manoeuvrings of the opposite sex, especially as those persons committing such obvious acts of emotional manipulation are probably not aware they are doing it. However, on a deeper subconscious level, they both suspect, albeit with an emotional intuition they are not prepared to share, that their spouse could well be more susceptible to the erotic imaginings of their disciples than they are to their own.

They both feel mature enough to recognise and control the urges stimulated into life by the activity of the limbic system. Surely, they reason, the newer more logical parts of the brain can acknowledge the impulses for what they are and suppress them. They love one another, they are a team, and whilst the sexual adventures of their younger days have long since passed, they have their spiritual connection - the soul sister, brother and lover who decided, pre-conception, to share their mortal existence on earth in each other's company. They are confident that the link that binds them together will remain securely in place. Nevertheless, the doubts that have now arisen do not willingly retreat in to the recesses of their daily life and their silent examination of their disciples' behaviour transcends into a comprehensive surveillance of each other's behaviour.

A life observed often appears more interesting than the one being lived by the observer. Consequently both husband and wife begin to believe the other is enjoying their daily existence more fully, and, experiencing much higher levels of personal inner self-contentment than they are individually.

There are so many assumptions to be made. And unless researched, validated and fully matured into objective facts, will remain exactly what they are – assumptions. A' what if 'un-validated remains where it is felt, rather than make the glorious transmogrification to the fully recognised reality of a 'What is'. A story carelessly created from a mass of assumptions very rarely reflects the glorious depths of reality personified – especially those associated with complex human relationships.

It was perhaps unfortunate then, that one day – a very significant day – he just happens to forget her birthday.

Birthdays are important to both of them. A birthday enables a period of total veneration and adoration to be experienced that is exclusively pertinent to the one person only. And let us be fair here - they are not alone in delighting in this uniquely personal validation which accompanies the celebration of an individual's emergence into the ongoing daily reality of human existence.

His leave of absence has been agreed in advance - the reason - he has been invited to a major international conference to lead a discussion on 'the efficacy of spiritual psychology in developing GDP within the world economy'. She does not wish to attend this conference as she finds the events where she is not invited to speak rather boring and inconsequential. He promises they will celebrate her special day over the whole of the following weekend. She, in accordance with the precepts of their religion (i.e. not to have a difficult conversation), acquiesces without making any particular fuss.

He is generally particular about keeping in contact with his wife whilst away from home, and he certainly has no intention of forgetting her on the actual day marking the anniversary of her arrival on the planet. However, on this one occasion, just as he is acknowledging the completion of a successful conference speech with his trusted disciples, fate - a concept that doesn't exist within the precepts of 'The Religion of Least Effort (RLE™)' - raises its inevitable multi-faceted head.

He only recognises the error of his absent mindedness when he looks at his cell phone, and, realising he has neglected to withdraw it from silent mode, sees he has missed twenty calls and has failed to respond to 15 text messages – each of which have got progressively more terse and intense as the period of his forgetfulness extends. At eleven in the evening he makes the equally fateful decision to call his wife, slightly the worse for wear following a possible surfeit of conference wine imbibed with his disciples in the corner of the hotel bar. The conversation lasts for all of fourteen and a half seconds. In the sixteen years they have lived together this is the first time she has ever expressed any anger towards him – and within those fourteen and a half seconds it would appear she was making up for lost time. She is furious. She feels belittled and un-important.

Obviously they have both experienced anger before, they are human after all. The point is their anger is generally articulated towards those others who, for one reason or other, have not behaved towards them in an acceptable way. Their justified anger will generally necessitate following the precepts of their own making which, as mentioned earlier, are contained within the ceremonial practices of 'The Religion of Least Effort (RLE™)', and involve cutting the perpetrator out of their life through performing the mandatory ritual entitled' the burning of the letter'.

When he returns home in time for their prescribed Weekly Dinner the atmosphere is dripping in condemnation. They have decided not to cook and have ordered an Indian takeaway. The lids on the foil containers holding their tarka dhal, bhindi bhaji, and chicken biryani remain tightly in place on the kitchen table. In silence the food resides patiently, waiting to be eaten. He places some serving spoons next to the foil containers, and, somewhat furtively, walks over to the fridge, opens the door and removes a chilled bottle of their special Bourgogne. He picks up an electric corkscrew from the sideboard and begins to unseal the bottle. His wife glares at him.

"I don't think you need to open that – we need to talk."

"I know we do but wouldn't a glass of wine help?" He looks away from her and places the electric corkscrew back on the sideboard where he had originally found it. He remains at the sideboard for several moments with his back to the wife, looking grudgingly at the wine bottle.

He can't ever remember being in a situation like the one he is currently experiencing. He is nervous and is beginning to realise he is actually scared of the woman he shares his life with. He feels an overriding sense of panic - of wanting to be anywhere else in the world rather than in the kitchen with this woman. He eventually turns around. She looks at him with lips quivering - the appropriate appearance of undiluted anguish pertinent to the intolerable circumstance she finds herself in.

"This is spiritual," she finally gasps as if struggling for breath." This is about the meaning that supports the truth of our life. This is about us - the spiritual consummation of our life. When did you start needing to drink from the vine in order to have a conversation with me? I don't think I know you anymore. You're not the man you once were. You've changed. You used to be so thoughtful - now you only ever think about yourself."

He observes his wife and notices for the first time she hasn't changed for dinner – but then again neither has he. She is wearing plain grey running slacks with pink stripes down the legs, an old cardigan wrapped around an equally tired 'The Religion of Least Effort (RLE™)' sweatshirt. He stares at his wife and the clothes she is wearing, momentarily lost in the stupor of his misery. She notices him looking at her attire in what she immediately considers to be a critical manner.

"No I haven't changed for dinner, I used to change for dinner when I had something meaningful and special to look forward to. I haven't anything to look forward to now. Whatever we had in the past has been destroyed hasn't it? Whatever it was between us has died."

She continues speaking before he has time to respond.

"I have had more than enough time to think and reflect on our life, and let me tell you I have been watching you carefully over the last few months. It's not just about my birthday - that bit of thoughtlessness on your part only confirmed my deepest suspicions. Over the last few days I have realised you have never given me anything. Everything I have achieved I have done through my own effort. You were never interested in my spiritual welfare. You are only interested in yourself."

All of a sudden he feels a wave of emotion build up in his body which starts flowing up and down from his toes to the crown of his head. It is not something he has ever experienced before and he certainly does not have the ability to contain the volcanic eruption of anger that explodes from his being. He looks at her and hates all he sees. He crashes both his fists on to the table and purposely knocks the containers of food onto the floor. He kicks them against the wall - Tarka dhal, bhindi bhaji, and chicken biryani spill out scattering as far as possible away from the couple. He turns on her with a voice filled with the scalding bitterness of his rage and spite.

"Oh really. Is that how you see our life together?" He pauses, "Well let me tell you what I see. This was always about you – it always has been. You and your precious little ego. I have more spiritual awareness in my little finger than you have in the whole of your body. At what point did you begin to believe you had become a saint within your own life time. People generally have to die first in order to be made a saint and you, my love, are anything but a saint. Your spirituality is as authentic as the face you hide behind your make up."

Silence... They look at each and yet see nothing. They are confused. The silence becomes too much. He closes his eyes, shakes his head in disbelief. His anger ebbs away.

"I can't deal with this – I want to be on my own. I don't need you or your help."

"I bet you don't, you have your precious disciple to help you."

The rage which had subsided begins to flow freely once more.

"What do you mean, my 'precious disciple'? I haven't a clue what you're talking about."

"Oh I think you do. Which one is it by the way - the blonde secretary? What a boring, mundane and predictable man you are - going off with the secretary." She smiles as she sees him sigh, believing she has just found the spark of truth in one of the many assumptions she has made.

He glares at her, screams in frustration, smashes his fists against the wall, walks over to the sideboard, picks up his car keys and walks out of the door, steps into the car, and drives for twenty miles before checking into a hotel for the night.

They separate formally shortly afterwards. One may have hoped it would have been an amicable parting of the ways, however this is not possible within the precepts of 'The Religion of Least Effort (RLE™)'. Instead, in separate rituals, observed by their disciples, they write their letters of disengagement from an un-productive relationship that prevents the growth of personal inner self-contentment - and ceremoniously burn them.

Regardless of the 'parting of the ways', life within 'The Religion of Least Effort (RLE™)'continues much as before. The business is too viable and productive to wind up and to do so would be extremely difficult and detrimental to the celebrity status they have both achieved - it is not an option. They decide to keep the news of their separation in-house, between themselves, their closest disciples, and their accountants and solicitors (who are more than happy to continue talking to each other even if their rich and profitable clients don't appear to be able to). They decide not to confess their marital difficulties to anyone else, including their celebrity friends, and, for no particular reason, their son.

They live the lie of their separation well - from outside appearances all continues to be normal. He continues speaking at his conferences and writing books, whilst she continues her training seminars and her spiritual agony aunt column. Quite naturally, as a result of their recent disappointments, his work begins to contain a degree of misogyny, whilst hers contains a distinct flavour of misandry. She continues to live in what was the marital home. He has moved in with one of his female disciples who just also happens to be his blonde personal secretary - of course it is a purely platonic arrangement.

It is exactly a year later when they accidentally meet again on the mid-morning chat show which is aired each weekday on national television. The researchers have not done their homework and so are delighted to get both founders of 'The Religion of Least Effort (RLE™) 'onto the one show. It is a bit of a coup since it is widely known that the two never normally agree to be interviewed together. This was a policy adopted many years ago and has nothing to do with their recent estrangement. They considered appearing together on the same show would somehow water down the amount of personal validation they would have received had they been appearing on their own.

When the arrangements are made with the individuals' secretaries the producers of the show forget to advise, and the secretaries neglect to ask, who the other guests will be - the producers naturally assume the couple are talking to each other. Neither of the guests, for they are actually the only ones booked for this show, are aware the other will be attending - their personal secretaries no longer communicate with each other over the content of their respective diaries.  They only realise they are appearing together when they meet in the green room prior to going on stage.

The host becomes aware of the icy tension between the two guests a few minutes prior to the commencement of the broadcast. As the show starts she is slightly apprehensive about what could transpire on air. She needn't have worried. As they answer her questions these bright young things, with master degrees and doctorates in the art of pure inner self-contentment, recognise, once again, the potential to join forces and save the World.

After the show they return to the green room. He reaches out and takes hold of her hand, squeezing it affectionately. He looks her in the eye and feels the rekindling of love spread through the whole of his body with the warm fuzzy haze of summertime.

"I nearly forgot how good we are together. What on earth happened to us?" He continues gazing at her affectionately. "I have really missed being with you. We are so good and right for each other. My life is only worthwhile with you in it. You know, we were joined together in heaven we should never have parted – we are meant to be. Let's get back together - together we can be so much more."

With tears beginning to appear in the corner of her eyes, she looks at him lovingly and sees her spiritual soul mate return to her bosom. He continues to speak.

"You know I will always be your action man, and you will always be my queen. Let's go on holiday together - have a second honeymoon, somewhere we have never been before, somewhere really exotic like..." He pauses. "Borneo – let's introduce 'The Religion of Least Effort (RLE™)' to East Asia. We've never been there before. It will be fun.

# Part 3 - The presence of the Vine

'On the outskirts of society you will see them walking listlessly outside, without and within, while you carry on working, nurturing the embodied soul'

In order for the vine to bear fruit it requires a fertile environment from which to draw nourishment - the fabric of life from which it sustains itself needs to be pliant with the flesh of its host willing.

If you have any concerns about whether or not you have been infected by the contagion that surrounds the vine, or that you are about to be contaminated, you need to determine just how fertile and pliant you are and whether or not you have created an environment conducive to its malignancy. Fortunately we can help you here. From our observations over the millennia the following emotional indicators correlate closest to the conditions in which the vine will thrive. This list is not exhaustive.

A feeling that life has passed you by, and that nothing you have done within society has ever had any real significance or value.

A sense that the society in which you subsist holds no purpose for you.

You feel at odds and in conflict with the values and beliefs of the other associate members who reside within the perimeters of your life.

That the funds from which you pay for your ongoing existence no longer serves a purpose as the currency of your existence.

A feeling of emptiness in all you do.

A desire to be on your own.

If you find yourself gravitating towards people who visibly display any of these symptoms assume you have been infected and take care. The vine thrives on emotional pain and likes to herd all its victims together into one location. Every emotional hurt you have ever experienced results in a scar and it is these scars from your past which provide gateways into the light of your present existence. Whilst a scar may seem to indicate you won't be hurt in the same place, invariably you will - simply because such wounds never fully heal. The more scars you bear the more fertile you have become over the years.

The vine can sense the emotional weakness of a potential host from a distance of many years. It will await patiently until pliancy is at its peak. This may occur at any time during the allotted span of your life on this planet. Whilst you may assume one would see the vine most clearly in the elderly of your species, don't be fooled into thinking you are safe. From our observations it appears that most people are infected by the age of thirty and whilst the vine may appear dormant – it is not – it activates itself through the distractions which make up your daily routine.

The vine is happy to bide its time and will lie seemingly dormant within the vicinity of its potential victims. It will creep around the doorways of your homes and before you realise it its tendrils will be pulling away the mortar and destroying the very fabric of your security. Likewise it lingers at the edges of your civilisation, encircling your villages, towns, cities and nation states. Its spores explore and navigates with ease through the atmosphere of your town halls and centres of government. Where there is corruption, disruption, discord and self-justification, you can be sure the vine is nearby. In every heated argument the vine will have an interest - for it enjoys the potentiality such interactions bring.

*********************************

# Chapter 7 – The Sailor

It is the wind that blows over the seas
That ripples the hearts of the lonely
And beckons them to come to me.

In the light of the early dawn he awakens in his bed to see the shadows of the leaves dancing on the ceiling. He pulls the duvet up over his chin and stretches his legs so that his feet dangle over the bottom edge of the mattress. He feels the cool air of the morning blow over his ankles and it is then that he has a sudden realisation. He is lonely. He feels an emptiness in his heart which extends beyond the vacant space and the unused pillow that occupies the area next to where he is currently lying. This emptiness extends across the upper hall way, down the stairs, into the kitchen and living area, through the back and front door and out onto the surrounding three quarter acre plot of land which serves as a garden for this home of his - a house that lies in the countryside on the edge of the suburbs of the city. He lies under the duvet for a few more minutes to consider just why he is even bothering to contemplate getting up and dressed – it is not as if he has got anything important to achieve, other than feed himself.

He raises himself from his bed, slides his legs to the floor and slowly brings his body to standing. As he stretches towards the ceiling into an upright position he notices his naked reflection in the mirror. With his eyes slowly focussing through the detritus of his sleep, he moves a few paces towards the full length antique French boudoir mirror – a memento from his last live in girlfriend who accidentally left it behind when, one morning five years ago, she suddenly decided for the sake of her own sanity she needed to vacate his life.

He stands to his full height, and scrutinises all he sees. He is not greatly impressed with the figure who looks back at him with slightly weak and bloodshot eyes. He observes a man who is clearly in his seventies, and whilst looking relatively fit and trim, he cannot fail to notice his skin looks slightly saggy and leathery, hanging off the skeletal frame as if it no longer has the motivation to fight the effect of the earth's gravitational pull. The reflection certainly does not match the self-image of the vibrant young man he visualises in his head – that person, it would appear, is no longer the reality of his physical existence. He removes the clothes he has allocated for his daily wear from the wardrobe and sits on the edge of his bed preparing to dress.

He sighs as he slips on his high street branded underpants, grey socks, tan tee-shirt, and light cream chinos. He stands up, moves back to the wardrobe and selects a crisply ironed blue Egyptian cotton shirt. He puts this on over the tee-shirt leaving it unbuttoned. He carefully rolls up the sleeves to his elbows. He inspects himself in the mirror and feels infinitely more at home with the reflection he now observes. He smiles and the apparition smiles back – ok he might be old, but boy oh boy he has had a good life, and there are certainly many more good times to come floating over the sea towards the horizon of his being.

The sailors 'good life 'can be summed up as three marriages, three divorces, six children (who don't speak to him but feel able to speak with each other), expensive divorce settlements - one of which still requires him to provide financial support for the youngest of his offspring, who is in her final year at The Boarding School) - and, finally, a long succession of girlfriends and illicit lovers who have proved to be equally expensive to maintain as his previous wives and children. Somewhere within all this he has managed a successful career in a leading professional service organisation.

He inherited the name 'The Sailor 'because he owned a 45 foot sailing boat - 'the ocean vine' - some ten years ago. This vessel was moored at a marina situated in the harbour of the seaside resort on the south coast. To be honest he wasn't a sailor at all and he certainly never qualified to be a skipper – if he moved the boat from its moorings he had to hire a 'friend'. Nevertheless he had spent most weekends on his boat dressed in the apparel he considered would give him the kudos of a seasoned man of the waves; for the boat was the ideal venue in which to entertain his illicit women acquaintances.

His third wife had guessed as much and enforced the sale of the 'ocean vine' as part of the settlement imposed on him during the acrimonious proceedings which followed the termination of their marriage. These proceedings were instigated somewhat speedily after she discovered him one Saturday afternoon, during a party to celebrate their wedding anniversary, in the marital bed lying on top of her best friend. That was ten years ago, nevertheless, he still enjoys recounting his seaward adventures when he has a suitably engaged audience, normally in the pub where he retires each lunchtime to enjoy his daily gin and tonic (with one mandatory ice cube) and have a natter with the boys.

He manoeuvres himself out of the bedroom, across the upper hall way, down the stairs, into the kitchen and living area, stopping on his way to pick up the three recently delivered daily newspapers lying on the front door mat. He places the newspapers on the coffee table adjacent to the settee and moves into the kitchen area where he prepares his breakfast - muesli moistened with a quarter pint of organic goats milk, two slices of wholemeal toast, and coffee.

Whilst he eats his muesli and takes tiny sips from a teeny cup of a piping hot espresso, his mind begins to meander across his past adventures when he was, in his opinion, a bright vibrant Adonis who every girl found attractive and, so they claimed, wished to 'sleep' with him.

Within an instant he is drawn far-away from his kitchen table, beguiled through the pleasant memories of his many romantic conquests, and there he remains, within his erotic imaginings, until a ray of sunshine flickers through the window and catches his eyes. He slowly, and reluctantly, begins to register the insistent knock on the door of his consciousness seeking an acknowledgement concerning the reality of his present existential condition. He returns from his amatory excursion to find himself holding a spoon containing muesli mid-air between the bowl on the table and his open mouth. All of a sudden he feels rather dejected

- the fantastical world were he had procreated with over a thousand women is far removed from  the operational reality of what now makes up his ordinary life on a daily basis.

After breakfast he gets out his lap top, logs on and checks into the various dating agencies he has taken up residence within. He finds his temporary online accommodation to be the cheapest and most effective way to identify companions with whom he can express his undying libido. The stress relieving act of copulation occurs much less frequently now since he has retired and no longer has the ready market of young things wishing to impress their future career underneath the sweat of his exerting loins. Following his retirement, and as he has got older, he has noticed with some degree of sadness and regret that the women who are inclined to meet up with him and share the secrets of his erotic imagination have also aged. He still persists however - he likes the challenge of meeting new women, and regardless of how ugly or old he finds them, there is always the chance that underneath the outer skin of what he finds personally abhorrent when the lights are on, there may be some wealth he can plunder through the guise of a long term relationship when the lights are off.

His reasoning is relatively simple. Not only does he need to satisfy the constant itch he feels in his groin, he is chronically short of the money required to live in the style he considers appropriate to his status. He has a wish to purchase a luxury apartment with a view overlooking the marina where he used to berth his boat. Although his house is currently on the market, and has been for the last five years, a wealthy woman who shares his dream and is prepared to pool her resources into the project could well help him achieve his goal sooner rather than later.

He doesn't feel any remorse about utilising a member of the fairer sex in this way and is relatively upfront and honest about his requirements within the various personal profiles posted on the dating agencies he is listed with. As far as he is concerned if he is lonely, the women he attracts will most probably be lonely, and he represents what can only be considered as a 'valuable catch'. He started using the dating sites more extensively after his last divorce and he is proud of his profile together with the portrait of himself in full skipper regalia on the prow of his boat. Nevertheless, he has still not yet met the woman of his dreams with the requisite wealth to consummate his long term ambitions.

The majority of his online adventures have resulted in an initial spell of unrequited love and lust followed very quickly by an increasing sense of ennui over the whole relationship thing. The woman seem pliant at first but then start making objectionable demands on his way of life. He likes to spend his time doing what he wants and doesn't see why he should compromise his joie de vivre to satisfy the irrational needs of the post menopausal. Consequently the emotional life of his relationships fizzle out before the light flickers on.

This of course leaves him with the ever constant dilemma of having to gratify his somewhat rampant libido unassisted by the delicate ministrations of others. This he achieves in the only way he knows how – a little personal self expression whilst observing, through the medium of his computer, acts of primal carnality undertaken between two or more people in front of a camera. He has never felt any remorse relieving his physical needs through the perusal of what he considers to be the natural behaviour of men toying with women; in reality he is rather proud of the fact that by doing this he has not yet succumbed to pacifying his personal tensions by paying for the privilege of a massage in the local city parlour. He does sometimes wonder whether the women he sees vocalising their orgasmic pleasure while the men practise a variety of sexual activities with them are actually enjoying themselves or just acting. However, such philosophical contemplation evaporates when he considers they are undoubtedly attaining some financial reimbursement for the privilege of doing something he rather personally enjoys doing for free - surely it must be more fun than having to work in a factory all hours of the day.

He checks the mail boxes on his dating sites and receives the reminder he is due to have a rendezvous with one of the latest little girlies he has been chatting to on-line. The thought of this cheers him up a little and drags him away from those morose early morning blues which were nagging annoyingly at the pleasures of his day. The two of them are due to meet this very evening at The Italian Cafe Bistro, a restaurant which has recently opened up in the city.

His potential conquest, who he has already mentally monikered as 'the bombshell blonde', excites him sufficiently enough to encourage him to spend a little time considering the sartorial arrangements for this particular occasion. He recognises the need to play his part well and present an image that will interest her enough to consider future liaisons with him. He hopes to woo her with sufficient enough charm so she will eventually agree to share some exercise with him, on a temporary basis at least, in the vacant half of his bed which has remained unoccupied much longer than his imagination would care to admit. As he brings into his mind's eye the potential of this upcoming encounter and considers it fully, he realises her profile is more than enough to make the average alpha male's blood temperature soar and make the heart beat significantly faster than is necessary for the healthy maintenance of life. He likes to think he is anything other than an average alpha male - as he will happily boast to his lady friends he is alpha extremis – a man's man, and indeed he does prefer the company of the male species whose manners and tastes he understands more readily than those of the female species. However, this preference for male company is frequently put to one side as and when he feels the need to recommence the 'chase' in order to satisfy the ever hungry urges of his libido.

According to her profile she is a natural blond, in her late thirties, 5' 11" in height, and, judging from the photograph, appears to be the proud possessor of original D cup bosoms. Her interests are athletics and sailing. She is a qualified accountant and a senior partner at a local firm some twenty miles from the outskirts of the city in which he lives. She is seeking someone to share excitement and adventure with - maybe more. As he examines the profile closely one more time he comes to the inevitable conclusion – he has the natural ability and skill to handle the goods being offered in a way that will provide ultimate satisfaction to all parties engaged in the transaction.

With this particularly pleasant thought in the forefront of his mind he trots upstairs to investigate his wardrobe. He decides an underlying nautical theme would probably be appropriate. He reaches inside the wardrobe and removes a cream linen suit with a double breast and brass buttons embossed with ships anchors. He carefully places the suit on the bed and returns to the wardrobe. For a moment he considers the selection of a traditional style Breton sailing shirt but thinks better of it and instead plumbs for the dark pink slim fit silk shirt with draw down collar. In order to reveal the true heights of his sartorial sophistication he has decided to wear a cravat and he has just the one suitable for the requirements of the evening. This cravat is pale yellow adorned with tiny golden ship anchors. There is matching silk kerchief that will be carefully placed in the breast pocket of the suit. To finish it all off he decides to give an airing to his faithful skipper's hat, which has a white crown and blue brim on which there is embroidered yet another golden anchor.

He resists the sudden urge to dress up in his selected clothes and peruse himself in the full length antique French boudoir mirror to confirm just how wonderful his appearance will be. He senses to do so would be childish and immature. He is confident in all matters concerning fashion and knows the young lady will be truly impressed. So instead he lays the clothes on his bed and returns downstairs, retrieves a jacket in the hallway, picks up the keys to the door and the keys for his car and leaves the house in search of a well-earned gin and tonic with the mandatory single cube of ice.

At around 12.30pm he arrives at the Four Feathers, deposits his vehicle on the weed infested rubbish filled car park, locks the door, and ambles through the entrance. Once within the threshold of the pub he makes his way over to the bar traversing the cigarette burnt, beer stained once colourful striped orange carpet. He orders his gin and tonic with the mandatory single cube of ice, settles himself on the bar stool, surveys the surroundings, and, with a nod of the head, acknowledges the existence of his fellow drinking companions.

"So the 'Young Un' is not honouring us with his presence again." He makes this remark as a statement of fact whilst still managing to imply a question that requires an answer to satisfy his immediate sense of curiosity.

"No, we think he's got hooked up with some of that pussy stuff he's always talking about – he's obviously practising his worship on the gloriously divine female." The informant starts chuckling, before continuing. "I saw him walking into his house the other week with some little bit of totty on hand – quite a looker she was – haven't seen him since." He gives the sailor a leery look and winks. "He's probably strained his old codger and can't walk."

"Well it was about bloody time he got a girlfriend, too much talk not enough action – a bit of good old rumpy bumpy will clear those cobwebs out of his brain. That's what I've always found. There is nothing like the exertion of the loins to keep your brain active."

The sailor smiles contentedly to himself as he reflects on the abundant possibilities for the future exercise of his loins that could well result from his liaison with the bombshell blond this very evening - providing, of course, he plays his cards with the professional aplomb he is more than capable of employing.

In the pleasure of his own thoughts he does not notice the smirk on the faces of his compatriots or their illicit winks and grins between one other. The sailor and his endless talk about women are amusing and keeps them relatively entertained when they are bored and have depleted all other interesting topics of conversation. Nevertheless it would appear women and the sexual adventures he has with them is the only subject he has any definitive opinion about, and to be quite honest, ongoing discourses with him are becoming a tad predictable.

The sailor misses the companionable qualities and conversational abilities of the 'Young Un', especially today when he so much news to share with him. The 'Young Un' is a man who appreciates the delectable arts required to fulfil the needs of female sensuality. He stares in silent contemplation, fixing his gaze on the slowly melting cube of ice in his glass of gin and tonic ,and falls into a daydream.

Then, just as suddenly, he jolts awake. He sits up straight and looks around. Feeling distinctly dissatisfied he begins to question what he is doing drinking in the bar of a dirty old dingy pub. He depressingly realises he has sat in the same spot virtually every lunchtime since he retired ten years ago, conversing and joking about his conquests over the opposite sex. He is no longer getting the looks of admiration and the jocular appreciation he deserves. He does a quick survey of his compatriots and considers the results. He arrives at a conclusion and passes judgement quickly - they are all old and bored with no life of their own worth talking about – he feels a sense of annoyance – no wonder he is not enjoying himself.

"Time to move out of the old peoples 'home and find some fresh green pasture to feed in," he says to himself as he quickly swigs down the remains of his gin and tonic, vacates the bar stool and the pub with just the briefest acknowledgement of farewell and adieu to his compatriots.

In the car park he suddenly feels a sense of alcoholic deprivation. He has drunk his gin and tonic too quickly and feels a momentary sense of loss. He considers driving over to the sixteenth century coaching inn he occasionally frequents when entertaining a new lady. He uses this slightly 'more upmarket' establishment after recognising the Four Feathers would not be a suitable venue for his particular brand of flirtation - the likelihood of being publicly acknowledged by his regular drinking companions would more than probably cramp his style, presenting an image not conducive for achieving the successful conclusion to his game of courtship. He grants his car permission to steer in the direction of the alternative hostelry and then, just as quickly, reverses his decision and heads back on the road that leads to his country residence.

It is approximately 3pm when he arrives back at the house and settles down on his large and extremely comfortable settee with another glass of gin and tonic with the mandatory single cube of ice. He picks up the newspapers placed on the coffee table earlier in the day and begins to read through the business and financial gossip. He always takes time to check the stocks and shares; it amuses him even though he no longer has any professional interest or investments worth talking about - the majority of them had been divested through his second divorce settlement. With the afternoon light flickering through the trees, making its way through the large patio windows creating shadows on the ceiling, he suddenly feels drowsy and falls asleep with his mouth open, emitting a strange though rather endearing purring sound of the kind generally associated with feline contentment.

He awakes with a jolt at 5.30pm. He hadn't really planned on falling asleep and now has only one hour to get himself prepared for his evening rendezvous. He has a sudden feeling of inner self-contentment as he knows, deep down inside his loins, his intimate evening soirée is going to go exceedingly well. It's not often a lady will agree to meet him on basis of several emails and a couple of phone calls. There is obviously an affinity between them, some magical chemical attraction that has leaked out and seeped its way ethernet-like through the broadband of his life. What he has particularly liked about their engagement so far is that there haven't been any of the embarrassing personal inquisitions over his past, or his age; she appears to have taken everything on his profile as a true reflection of who he is and what he wants – likewise he has chosen to take everything she has written about herself with the same degree of trust.

In a sudden attack of anxiety he contemplates momentarily whether or not he has been too hasty in applying his hard earned trust to a woman he hardly knows anything about. Then he relaxes as he remembers that most of their conversations have focussed on her professional work. They had shared quite a few amusing anecdotes about life in the world of professional services. It is obvious that the attraction she must already feel towards him is as a result of his experience in business, which is in fact very similar to hers. He has always been a excellent judge of character and his initial feelings about a person are generally right – she will be a 'goodun' - she appears attractive, she is financially independent and she could well be the first women he dates who has an intellectual capability commensurable to his.

With this happy thought in mind he trots back upstairs to his bedroom, carefully removes his clothes, putting his underpants and socks into the dirty linen basket, and carefully hanging the other clothes on their respective hanger in the wardrobe. As he turns to walk to the bathroom he sees his reflection again in the ex-girlfriends full length antique boudoir French mirror. He is momentarily annoyed his reflection is demanding attention and diverting him from undertaking the important preparations required for the evening. However he pauses, takes a couple of steps toward the mirror, and for the second time in the day, takes a moment to consider and admire the full glory of his naked torso.

"Not bad, even if I think so myself," he addresses this remark towards his reflection whilst swinging his body through a 180 degree revolution. His penis dangles and sways gently from left to right. "You never know, my boy, even you may get some action later." He addresses this last remark towards his penis, and chuckles, "you won't be flopping around much then, will you?"

He takes a little more time to inspect the full fabric of his ship and pass judgement on whether or not it is in adequate shape for the evening's voyage. Well, he certainly isn't fat, yet neither is he thin. The hair covering his body is now coarse, white and somewhat long. He decides it could well be a good idea to give it a trim before going out. He also notices, somewhat ruefully, that the almost full head of sandy coloured hair he possessed five years ago is now completely white and has substantially decreased in quantity. Unfortunately this has made the dome of his head look like a mountainous pink island surrounded by white water waves crashing and breaking in upon the shore. He has recently had it cut short and whilst he would have preferred the full head of hair he acknowledges the new look is one of distinction and gravitas. He chooses to ignore the flesh hanging loosely from his arms and buttocks – this is of no importance – she won't have to see him naked, he will be fully clothed, and, if anything is likely to happen, it will be with the light off. In all fairness to the sailor he does not generally expect any sexual adventures to transpire from a first date - he just likes teasing himself with the idea of it. He goes into the bathroom, fills the tub with hot water and a little scented oil, and spends the next twenty minutes or so scrubbing and cleansing every part of his visible anatomy. After drying himself he rubs a little scented oil over his remaining hair, sprays his whole body with scent, brushes and flosses his teeth, and, finally, rinses his mouth with a gargle of mint wash.

He takes fifteen minutes to dress carefully, ensuring each piece of apparel is positioned optimally to create the image he wishes to portray. He starts with a pair of navy designer underpants – an occasion like this does not warrant high street branded clothing and he always remembers the old adage, 'you can tell the jib of the man by the clothes he wears'. Like-wise the socks are not any old socks – this is a brand new pair brought from a reputable tailor in the city, black with golden anchors stitched into the sides. He then decks himself out in the clothes he set out earlier, checks himself in his ex-girlfriends full length antique boudoir French mirror, runs his hand over his bald dome and smoothes down his hair. He smiles giving himself full marks in appreciation for what he has achieved. Picking up his faithful skipper's hat, he runs down stairs, and purely for the purpose of maintaining his self-confidence, pours himself a medicinal gin and tonic with the mandatory single cube of ice. He drinks it down in a gulp and tips the remaining ice cube from the glass into the sink. He puts on his shiny black dress shoes and gives them a quick wipe around with the tea cloth from next to the sink – for as another old adage reminds him, 'you can judge the man by the state of his shoes'. He picks up his car keys, vanishes through the front door into the cool evening air, jumps into his car, and, drives into the city.

He parks his car on a street close to The Italian Cafe Bistro, walks a couple of hundred yards up the side street opposite the river and walks through the front door at approximately 7.20pm. Once inside a waiter acknowledges his presence with the formality of a courteous greeting and takes the sailor to the table which has been reserved in his name. The blonde is due to meet him here at 7.45pm, however he has arrived early so he can settle himself down with a pre-dinner gin and tonic. He sits at the chair and takes a moment to fully appraise and take stock of his surroundings.

From the outside it has to be said that The Italian Cafe Bistro does not look particularly Italian being housed as it is in a former public house. The exterior walls of the lower storey have been painted black and the upper storeys painted white. The original pub windows have been removed and four large plate glass windows have extended over and beyond the width and height of the originals. As you look towards the front of the building there are three windows to the left of the door and one to the right. In front of the right hand side window there are two bistro coffee tables housing ash trays and four metal frame chairs which, by the state of their appearance, are doing their utmost to discourage anyone from sitting outside. Above the original pub door is a large sign emblazoned in gold paint identifying the premises as The Italian Cafe Bistro.

The inside decor, however, does its utmost to encourage patrons to believe they are about to dine in an authentic restaurant set in Italy rather than in a refurbished public house in the city. The original bar has been removed along with all the internal walls that used to separate the snug from the saloon and the saloon from the lounge. This creates a large dining room with three separate serving areas. The ceiling is covered with the banners of famous Italian football teams, and they have hung bunting in the green, white and red of the Italian national flag on the beams supporting the ceilings where the dividing walls once stood, Whilst the walls appear to be decorated in the original crimson paint, which served duty when the establishment was still a hostelry, neither the colour nor the aged nature of the paint can be seen clearly as they are covered from top to bottom with stretched canvas frame black and white photographs of Italian native residents eating vast quantities of pasta in a variety of famous cities and rural locations.

The sailor sits at a table set for two persons in what was probably the saloon area, facing the door so he can observe all who enter. The waiter is a tall young man with a thick mop of black hair expertly slicked back over the top of his head and tied into a small pony tail. He is dressed in the black trousers and white shirt generally associated with Italian waiters, and indeed he looks Italian and remains so until he speaks. When he does the illusion of heredity is broken; he has the strong regional accent associated with a person born and bred in the West Country. Nevertheless, as far as the sailor is concerned, he appears to be polite and attentive.

"Are you dining alone tonight sir?" He asks.

"No, I am waiting for a young lady to join me; she will be here at 7.45pm."

"Can I get you something to drink while you wait?"

"Ummm, yes, could I have a double gin and tonic, with a slice of lemon and one cube of ice?"

"Of course sir, coming up right away."

The waiter returns with a tumbler in which there resides a double gin, slice of lemon, and, one cube of ice. A bottle of Indian tonic water stands next to the tumbler with its top removed. The waiter places the glass and bottle on the table well within the grasp of the sailor, neglecting to pour the tonic into the tumbler. He then moves to the side of the restaurant and returns with a couple of menus. He hands them to the sailor and advises that the 'specials of the day 'are marked up on the various chalk boards dotted strategically around the walls in between the pictures. Everything on the menu is available this evening with the exception of the sea bream, which is 'off'.

The sailor settles down with his drink, the menu, and waits.

At 7.40pm he takes out his cell phone and calls the number the bombshell blonde has given him. It immediately goes onto her answer message.

"That's good," he thinks to himself, "she must be on her way." He places the phone back in his pocket and continues to sip his gin and tonic. He notice the ice cube has nearly melted.

At 7.45pm he orders another double gin with a slice of lemon and one cube of ice. He doesn't order any more tonic as half the original bottle still remains to be drunk. He takes his cell phone from his pocket, checks it is switched on, and places it on the table where he can see it. He starts an initial perusal of the menu so he can make his personal recommendations to the bombshell blonde about the dishes she may care to partake of.

By 7.50pm he has decided on a main course of stuffed baked lobster. It is the most expensive item on the menu and he is sure the bombshell blonde will be impressed, firstly by the lobster choice itself, and secondly, because he hasn't gone for one of the cheaper dishes on the menu. He has a few ideas about a starter, but will wait for the bombshell blonde, as a discussion over food choices is always a great way, as they say, 'to break the ice'. He grins to himself and begins to peruse the selection of fine wines The Italian Cafe Bistro has to offer.

Over the next ten minutes he starts to feel a sensation of anxiety touched with an additional pinch of frustration and annoyance - he keeps looking towards the door and checking his phone for any message.

The restaurant is not particularly busy tonight – only two tables of four inhabited by youngsters who appear to have come straight to the Italian Cafe Bistro from a busy work day at the office. Nevertheless their laughter, drinking, eating and sense of bonhomie, provides fuel to the fire of his increasing sense of irritation. He hears a phone ring and, although the ringtone is different to his, he immediately checks his phone. A few minutes later the waiter walks over to his table with what can only be described as a look of pity pasted over with an inauthentic expression of professional concern. The waiter stands at the side of the sailor and, without making eye contact, delivers the message.

"Sir, I regret to inform you I have had a call from your young friend asking me to tell you she has been caught up unavoidably with business and will not be able to join you tonight. She asks that you don't contact her; she will contact you when she is free. I hope this won't stop you from enjoying your meal. Shall I leave you for a few minutes and come back and take your order?" Without waiting for an answer the waiter walks off to the other side of the restaurant and starts talking and laughing with one of the tables of youngsters. The sailor can't be sure but he senses they are all looking over in his direction and that their current discourse is about him.

As a personal sense of paranoia starts to take over his emotional state, he feels completely humiliated and rather angry at the simple lack of courtesy afforded him by the bombshell blond and the waiter. His appetite vanishes and with a sudden burst of temper, walks up to the till, demands the bill from a rather shocked waiter, pays it in full and walks out of the The Italian Cafe Bistro neglecting to provide even the smallest of financial tips for the service he has received.

He returns home at around 8.50pm and immediately pours himself a large gin and tonic with the mandatory cube of ice, retrieves his lap top, and logs on immediately to the dating site where he met the bombshell blonde. He is too angry to ring her, but is interested to see if she has bothered to post a message for him. She hasn't.

He opens her profile page eager to check her listing and see what impediment he must have obviously missed when making his personal assessment of her suitability as a companion. As he does so he glances at the members forum - the space in which members can share news and gossip, there he notices a message written at 8.36pm by the bombshell blond for all to see.

*'OMG, early night for me - as always it was too good to be true. I have just had a lucky escape. Beware the man calling himself 'the sailor'. His profile is not to be believed. Look at his picture and I am sure you will see why I was interested in meeting him. Well I can confirm the picture was not*

*taken any time during this century. I arranged to meet him at The Italian Cafe Bistro at 7.45pm. As always, I arrived late so I could inspect the date through the windows. Well instead of seeing the Adonis whose profile picture adorns his listing page, imagine my shock and horror when I spied this bald old saggy man who was probably older than my grandfather. How could he think I would be interested in a personal relationship with someone old enough to be my grandfather? As for his dress sense, you would have to see it to believe it. I am still suffering from the shock – seriously - he was wearing a pink shirt, yellow cravat, a yellow kerchief in his breast pocket, a double breasted suit with brass buttons (I ask you), and finally - get this - a captains hat with an embroidered anchor was lying next to him on the table. I doubt he has had access to a woman of any taste for some years. Anyway, beware, I spoke to him on the phone and he comes across quite plausibly.'*

He reads the posting and then he re-reads it. It takes him over two long minutes for it to sink in that the posting actually relates to him. He feels his heart start to pound as a wave of shock emanates from his feet rushing to his head and then returning back and forth like the ebb and flow of the sea against a rocky shore line. He sits stunned, unable to believe what has happened. Little sobbing noises erupt from his throat, and for the first time in many years he starts to weep. Tears rush down the sides of his cheeks and a long string of phlegm starts moving its way out of his nose on to his lower lip.

He leaves the gin and tonic with the single cube of ice on the table, shuffles through the kitchen door, down the hallway passage, up the stairs and into his bedroom where he slowly removes his suit and places it on the requisite hanger in the wardrobe, takes off his shirt, underpants and socks, discarding them into the linen basket. He moves towards the double bed and stares at it morosely. He slides under the duvet and lies on the right hand side of the bed curled up in the foetus position clutching his penis with his left hand and sucking the thumb of his right hand.

In the light of an early dawn he awakens to see the shadows of the leaves dancing on the ceiling. He pulls the duvet up over his chin and stretches his legs so his feet dangle over the bottom edge of the mattress. He feels the cool air of the morning blow over his ankles and it is then he has a sudden realisation. He is lonely. He feels an emptiness in his heart which extends beyond the vacant space and the unused pillow that occupies the area next to where he is currently lying. This emptiness extends across the upper hall way, down the stairs, into the kitchen and living area, through the back and front door and out onto the surrounding three quarter acre plot of land that serves as a garden for this home of his - a house which lies in the countryside on the edge of the suburbs of the city. He lies under the duvet for a few more minutes to consider just why he is even bothering to contemplate getting up and dressed – it is not as if he has got anything important to achieve, other than feed himself.

# Chapter 8 – The Philanthropist

'The value of what you give
can only be measured by
the monetary value of that you receive in return.'

A s he sits at the head of the table situated within the building he likes to think of as his feasting hall, five minutes prior to delivering his speech, he momentarily forgets the name of the charity he is representing tonight. He is the patron of several, and due to the similarity of their particular aims and objectives, and his increasing age, he sometimes suffers an understandable degree of amnesia regarding the specific details in the speech he is required to make.

The momentary lapse in concentration annoys him as it is a matter of immense personal pride that he can speak to an audience without notes. This is not due to any particular improvisational skills (although some are obviously involved); it's just that he has, through the dedication of many hours practice, learnt by heart the key themes and structure of his 'charity 'speeches. He only has to fill in the missing elements of his address from information regarding the charity's recent good works and social successes. These particulars are derived from the data supplied to him on the day by the relevant incumbent chief executive. This additional knowledge is normally basic enough to be learnt and held securely within his once impeccably efficient short term memory on the actual day. He then uses the face of the chief executive as a mnemonic anchor to remember who and what he is talking about.

Unfortunately this evening, as he turns around to remind himself which particular chief executive is residing in the seat reserved for a person of such an august position, he notices it is currently empty.

Although for the sake of this particular story we have called him the philanthropist, if you should happen to meet him at one of the many functions in which he chooses to network you will be required to call him

Sir. For indeed he is a Knight of the Realm for services rendered to charity, and although not specifically receiving the shoulder strokes from the sword of the majesterial one herself, accepted them from the naturally appreciative and respectful rightful heir to the throne who, on that particular day at the palace, had been given the right and responsibility to do so. For this reason and this reason only, and because he himself would insist on it anyway, we are going to grant him an honorific capital letter P in front of his name to recognise the sacrifice of a career given over to the service of himself, and, of course, others.

He is an alumnus of The Boarding School has an unwavering faith in the proposition contained within the School's latin motto -' You will be valued by what you contribute to society'. This was also the view held by his father who had frequently told him,

'Don't ever forget where you came from boy! Always give to the world and the world will give back to you. You will know if you have done well through the level of recognition and respect given to you by your peers'.

Owing to the regularity in the delivery of this sermon, and the ongoing indoctrination of The Boarding School whilst he was a student there, this particular belief has come to underpin his behaviour towards all he aspires. It has also ultimately resulted in this particular evening's charity networking dinner, which is given and provided for the up and coming business people of the principal locality in which he resides. It is an area his family have been associated with for some time. His father, within the duration of an extremely long life, had been appointed, 'President of the Local Traders Association '(ten continuous years), city councillor, county councillor, and finally, Alderman of the rather over populated city in which they then lived. When his father died over five hundred people crammed into the small provincial cathedral for a memorial service led by the local suffragan bishop.

After the Philanthropist left The Boarding School he was accepted into an Oxbridge College. At university, with his father's categorical disapproval, he read Economics and Strategy within Business, and to spite him ensured he was awarded a degree with first class honours. Throughout his early years the Philanthropist's every move was curtailed by having to live in the shadow of his father's greatness. It was hardly surprising, therefore, that in order to remove himself from the insufferable negativity his father cast over all his hopes and ambitions, he excused himself from the family home as soon as he was financially viable. This occurred as a result of achieving in excess of 85% in his final marks. He was headhunted onto the fast track graduate management programme for a large reputable international engineering firm. It was about this time he met the young lady who would later become his very attractive wife. Father and son became estranged and were only finally reconciled when the father was laid out in the coffin awaiting his funeral.

He rose rapidly through the managerial ranks of the reputable international engineering firm and in the space of four years was appointed to fulfil to a new and vital role within the business. His responsibilities were set out within the personal specification attached to the seemingly important job description entitled: 'International Director of Innovations and Futures (new post)' - he was was to assemble a team of equally intelligent young entrepreneurs with terms of reference to develop innovative ideas and products that would safeguard the future of the business.

Unfortunately the senior executive board failed to grasp why they had created the new post in the first place. Clearly they thought by just establishing the role, especially one with such a dynamic job title, the future of their business was now secure. So when the Philanthropist and his team revealed the depth of their intellectual capacity and proposed a truly radical product that would corner a market previously un-perceived by lesser mortals such as themselves, they were somewhat offended and rejected the scheme out of hand. The Philanthropist took the rejection well - in fact he took it with a smile as he and half of his team handed in their notice and set up a small manufacturing unit on a medium sized industrial estate situated in the countryside just ten miles from the city of his birth. Together with his team he proceeded to do exactly what they had proposed to the senior executive board – corner the market with a radically new product.

This was over forty years ago and the rest, as we would say, is history – the company went on to become an internationally best-selling brand and was publicly listed on the stock market some twenty five years later. This was shortly after he had bought, just to prove a point, the reputable engineering firm where his own career had first started. Ten years on the Philanthropist, who was then only known as the Chairman and Chief Operating Officer, chose to accept a payoff presented to him by the principal shareholders, retire and cash in all his options. As a result he acquired a mere £580 million to play with and use as he saw fit, without having to justify any of his decisions to a company board or to a group of 'bloody useless shareholders'.

He decides to put his £580 million to work by becoming a Business Angel – funding start-up businesses he believes will be profitable, and helping their owners through networking opportunities and the personal endorsement of their products. At the same time he also establishes a charitable trust directing and managing a variety of fund raising activities to provide additional resources of finance for a selection of charities associated with the search for a cure to the various forms of cancer the world is inflicted with.

His initial reason for operating within the voluntary sector was to achieve a goal his father would have been jealous of – an Order of the British Empire (OBE) - his father, only ever having achieved an MBE, had never felt truly recognised for his 'good' works to society.

Nevertheless the Philanthropist was quite surprised to achieve his own goal within couple of years. Needing a new objective to motivate him and really snook one up the nose of his deceased father – he decided to become a Knight of the Realm. This he achieved two years ago and the 8' by 5' oil painting, which hangs in the gables opposite to where he is currently sitting, celebrates the occasion.

In reality his feasting hall is nothing more than a large converted stone warehouse attached to the Georgian manor house and farm he and his wife purchased and restored some thirty years ago. The whole site came with approximately 1,000 acres of land which he rents out to a local farmer nearby. They kept the house, outbuildings, and the two acres of land - in which his wife created the formal gardens. The outbuildings have been converted for domestic purposes and now accommodate a large office and meeting room, fitness suite, garage, and the feasting hall.

The feasting hall is relatively large being 70' in length, 30' in width, and 40' in height to the apex of the ceiling. The walls, up to the height of what would have been the original internal ceiling prior to being removed by the Philanthropist, are panelled with dark oak in the Victorian style redolent of an Oxbridge college dining hall. From that height upward the remaining walls are rendered with a white wash up to the wooden ceiling, which is itself supported by an intricate design of antique oaken trusses. Whilst this may sound somewhat stark and old fashioned, the appearance is ameliorated by the the pictures and sculptures of a modern temperament hung from the oak panelling.

These pieces are of a mid-range quality in terms of artistic achievement and priced accordingly at between £1,000 and £3,000. One of his latest 'projects' as a business angel is the role of dealer for an artist who wanted to establish a gallery catering for middle level professionals. The Philanthropist has obliged the artist by allowing the Feasting Hall to be used for private viewings. At the same time he has financed the design of a sophisticated virtual online gallery and auction house where members of the public and commercial world can purchase the art required for maintaining an appearance of sophistication without the tedious need to visit one. In the meantime he charges the artist a thirty percent commission on anything he sells in the feasting hall 'gallery 'whilst awaiting for the loans he has provided the artist to be repaid with interest.

The placements for this evening's dinner have been selectively laid out for the benefit of the one hundred and fifty privileged guests. These carefully chosen invitees are now installed alongside the double row of trestle tables traversing the whole length of the room. These trestles are brought together at the top of the hall by an adjoining' head 'table crossing the dividing width between them. This, unlike the trestles, is an old oak dining table of significant size, and, sitting higher above the rest, denotes the seat of importance and power.

The fact that the dining area is primarily assembled from 6' metal trestle tables is not immediately apparent for they are dressed from top to bottom in extravagant Egyptian cotton and furnished with equally overstated dining ware. This gives the trestles together with their occupants ideas and thoughts way above their ordinary station in life.

The Philanthropist sits at the centre of the large oaken table looking down at the diners and towards the portrait celebrating his knighthood. This wonderful picture was the creation of his ward who thoughtfully painted it for him two years before he actually received the honour.

The lady mayor of the nearby city is sitting on his left, and the chief executive of the charity being honoured at this dinner, should be sitting at his right hand side. Unfortunately this particular chief executive is still absent from the seat of honour.

The seating arrangements for the remainder of the dining area is simple – the richer you show yourself to be, (measured by the size of donation you make), the closer towards the head of the table you will be seated. So the very wealthy will be sat, according to what he considers to be a worthy and fine medieval tradition, 'above the salt', and the less wealthy, (he doesn't invite anyone who has no wealth to show off), will sit below the salt, alongside any of the charity's administration team who have been instructed to help with the organisation of the dinner and inform would be financial backers what the charity actually does. He makes no secret of his policy - the Philanthropist is not a man known for hiding behind his own metaphors - and there are two large ceramic salt cellars placed on each row between the half way and three quarter point towards the head table. These are placed at the whim of the Philanthropist depending on his mood on the day. It has become something of a local competition for invitees, competing with their acquaintances and neighbours to see how far beyond 'the salt 'they can go.

The Philanthropist particular enjoys running this type of charitable networking event - he is aware everyone in the room, regardless of where he has sat them, is wealthy and willing to show off their spending power. He doesn't even need to do any direct selling; his invitation has done all the hard work for him. At least 25% of the attendees will buy a piece of art off him before the end of the evening, under the mistaken belief, not even promulgated by himself, that the profits will be going to charity. And as most of them will display the innate emotional need endowed within the psyche of humanity to ingratiate themselves before figures of wealth and authority, they won't even enquire as to where the money is going. He will not, of course, feel any compunction to tell them. This keeps everyone happy.

He is increasingly conscious the chief executive's seat is still vacant, and there are now only a couple of minutes before he is due to start his speech. He looks down the hall with a certain degree of irritation, to see if he can locate the chief executive. The problem is, for the moment at least, he can't even remember who the person is or what they look like. He turns towards the lady mayor thinking of possible ways he can ascertain which charity is 'being honoured', without letting on he has had a temporary lapse of cognitive functioning. He decides to say nothing. It's at times like this he wishes his wife was next to him; she always had a good memory for everything.

The Philanthropist still doesn't quite understand why his wife left him. This happened sometime ago. He had arrived home at 9.00 pm and everything was as he expected it to be - well nearly. The candles had been lit on the central granite kitchen island where they dined, the music was playing, and the air smelt of cooked onion and garlic. However the table had not been set out for three people, i.e. for himself, his wife and the one daughter who still lived at home. Instead there was one place set with a plate covered by another plate together with a note explaining this was his 'après networking supper' which could be reheated by placing the plates in the microwave. His wife also helpfully explained where the microwave was situated - on the kitchen work top underneath the window.

The fact was then, as it still is today, networking equates with business success, and whilst he would have accepted he was enjoying increasingly lengthy drinking sessions with clients and colleagues in the pub, this was essential to the success and the prosperity of his business and their family life. He had thought his wife understood that.

It was later the same evening he discovered the other letter saying she had 'had enough 'of being his 'little shadow 'and wanted to live a life dedicated to her own interests – she had gone, with their eighteen year old daughter, to stay with her parents.

For some reason they never got back together. Neither did they get divorced. After the initial shock wore off, their separation appeared quite natural and they have remained on relatively good speaking terms ever since. She still maintains the gardens whilst he provides her with a more than generous annual allowance. Whilst he will always ask his wife about her 'interests', he is is not particularly interested in, and has never really understood, what her 'interests 'are. To be quite honest, the only activities that have ever really concerned him relate to making money and enhancing his position within society.

However, since the separation from his wife he has taken a greater interest in his ward. This 'son 'was bequeathed into his guardianship following the death of his very good friend and former school compatriot. The Philanthropist ensured the boy remained at The Boarding School and followed in his own footsteps towards a career in business. The boy did and attained a first class honours degree in business strategy and economics from the very same Oxbridge college the Philanthropist attended.

Initially the Philanthropist had not been interested in having much of a relationship with the boy. Whilst the girls were at home he wasn't prepared to allow the remotest risk of teenage testosterone to jeopardise his daughters 'future. Consequently the boy was never encouraged to join in with the family life at the 'manor'. Now, however, he feels as a father to a son, and considers him as one of his own. Another of his part time hobbies has been sorting out the affairs of his deceased friend's business - part of the legacy they bequeathed to their son. He is proud of the fact he has developed the business into a profitable international company which is now managed by his ward

For those of you who are curious about such matters it is probably worthwhile to take a moment to describe the physical appearance of our Philanthropist. It would be erroneous to make assumptions about his mien, therefore some foreknowledge of his comportment could be considered useful. Appearances can be deceitful and should you meet the Philanthropist you may not immediately recognise him for what he truly is. This would be an unfortunate miscalculation on your part. So for your benefit; he is 5' 8" in height, relatively stout but without revealing anything that could be described as a paunch. He has a thick main of white hair that rests on his shoulder, and a large white handle bar moustache that hangs underneath an equally large bulbous nose. It is hard to define any particular facial features as one's attention is generally drawn to his piercing blue eyes and then to the moustache, without necessarily noticing anything else. He dresses in indigo jeans on all occasions, except notably, on his wedding, and the day at the palace when he was made a Knight of the Realm - at each event he was required, and he acquiesced, to wear a dark morning suit. His shirts tend to be of the chequered variety, he eschews any form of neck wear and he favours tweed jackets.

He is clever, astute, and has an immense belief in his own ability to make money. He does not tolerate anyone who disagrees with his personal values. He is acerbic, quick to temper, and used to getting his own way. He is a socialist who always votes conservative; an imperialist who believes in Europe; and a monarchist who believes in a republic. He despises politics as a profession and, with the exception of the lady mayor, refuses to entertain politicians at any social event he is organising. He has his own ideas as to how the country should be run and is more than prepared to share them if anyone is careless enough to invite an opinion. He says what he sees and is proud of his forthrightness. Should anyone consider him rude, he really doesn't care ' –business is business', and his whole life has been dedicated to it. If necessary he is more than happy to swear profusely at a person if it shocks them into reality – his reality.

His attention is momentarily caught by the Humulus Lupulus hop vines which have been hung along the dado rails separating the mock Victorian oak panelling and the white washed wall. They were the gift from a local grower, now in her early seventies, whose husband - an old acquaintance of his - had died of a heart attack many years back. She and her replacement husband had sold their lucrative legal practice and taken over the running of the farm - something about quality of life - another concept he doesn't really understand. They are now regular supporters of his charitable trust - her daughter had tragically died at the relatively young age of forty six with cancer of the liver. They are seated just above the salt on the right hand side from where he is sitting. He looks over towards them and feeling a sudden rare and unexpected pang of compassion, catches their attention and smiles at them in an acknowledgement of their existence.

Yes – he has been worrying about his health lately. Possibly because of the red veins which have started appearing all over the surface of his face; the shortness of breath he is starting to experience as he walks around the grounds; the change in the shape of his nose; the numbness he feels occasionally in his feet; and the forgetfulness that means he can't remember the name of the bloody charity he is acting as host for tonight. He is beginning to fear the advent of his death, so instead of going to a doctor for a medical MOT, he has started attending the local parish church. As he has come to learn through his regular presence at the

Sunday morning services held at 10.30am each week, altruism is in fact his saving grace – and as everybody knows he is extremely altruistic.

He looks around again and confirms the chair next to him is still silently vacant and devoid of the person who is supposed to be sitting there. Doesn't the chief executive have the courtesy or respect to realise his presence is expected, not only by him but also by his guests. The chief executive is supposed to be sat in that particular seat so he can look admiringly and indicate his appreciation towards the Philanthropist as he makes his speech. He suddenly feels even more irritated when he remembers he has agreed to sponsor the whole event. He can't remember why he consented to this – it is not his usual style at all. Yes he lets the charity have the feasting hall free of charge; yes, he will arrange the publicity and send out the invitations; yes, he will act as host - but tonight he has even agreed to hire the caterers. He feels a sudden sense of resentment – all these people are being entertained and fed at his own expense, paid for from the money he has earned through the hard labours of his life. Is it cost justifiable, he asks himself, will he ever get a return on his investment?

He looks at his watch. It's nearly time to call order and start his evening address. There is finally no choice – he turns to the lady mayor, who, in the absence of a wife, takes the role of consort at these occasions.

"What are we actually doing this for?"

He has known the lady mayor for over ten years. She has an interest in the same sort of philanthropic endeavours as he does. They met at a networking event in support of a charity they had both just agreed to be trustees for. He likes the fiery feisty temperament that matches her strikingly dyed dark red hair. She, in return, rather enjoys his belligerent disposition that fully compliments her somewhat earthy whit.

The lady mayor assumes his question is rhetorical - she herself was just contemplating the amount of time she spends attending events such as these. Nevertheless she replies.

"Because we believe in the cause we are supporting? And haven't you always said 'Curing Cancer for Everyone 'is one of the more effectively run organisations you have had the privilege of working with? Of course you may be biased."

He doesn't quite understand what she is inferring by her response so gives a perfunctory grunt by way of acknowledgement. At least he knows the name of the organisation even if he can't remember the name of the chief executive. No matter, he will just refer to him by his job title, chief executive, and make up the rest. He lifts himself from the chair into an upright position, switches on the lapel microphone power unit, which is fastened to the belt of his jeans, picks up a spoon and bangs it loudly upon the oaken table, waits for a respectful silence, and then, only then, begins his speech.

"Dear Honourable Lady Mayor, ladies, gentlemen and miscellaneous others, on behalf of myself and the chief executive, wherever he happens to be."

He pointedly stares at the empty chair beside him,

"I would like to thank you for attending our little networking soiree this evening..... Now unaccustomed as I most obviously am to public speaking,"

he pauses to savour the ripple of laughter his self-deprecating joke is designed to illicit,

"it is incumbent on me to speak to you on behalf of......."

He pauses and looks around the room as if seeking someone in particular,

"myself,"

he pauses again to allow the little ripple of laughter to spread its way around the room and dissolve on its journey towards the apex of the roof, "and on behalf of Curing Cancer for Everyone - the charity you are supporting tonight by paying for the pleasure of attending this - my little networking evening......."

He pauses yet again and looks around the room with a serious expression on his face.

"As a successful business man who knows what he is talking about, may I encourage you to do exactly that, i.e. network over the coffee and brandy that will be served after I have finished speaking in approximately forty minutes time."

He pauses yet again for the laughter that will inevitably come when the audience realises what he has just said and then realise it is a joke, for you see none of his speeches ever last longer than ten minutes.

"It was at opportunities like this when I made the majority of contacts who encouraged and enabled my success as an entrepreneur and contributed to the wealth I now use for charitable purposes such as this. So please use this opportunity I have given you to mingle, to catch up with old friends and hopefully make some new ones.

For the next few minutes I would like to share some of my own personal experiences of the business world that will hopefully emphasise the importance of what we bring, as the business community, to causes such as Curing Cancer for Everyone. Quite simply without us they would cease to exist. The economic and political environment in which they operate needs the business nous that we as individuals can bring. This is why I throw my somewhat considerable weight,"

he pauses again for the expected and duly received peals of laughter,

"my considerable weight behind charities such as Curing Cancer for Everyone. My dear late father, an Alderman for our nearest and dearest city, who, I should add, was nearly as successful as myself, often told me. 'Never ever forget where you come from boy. Always give to the world and the world will give back to you.' This is the underlying principle by which I have lived my life...............''

He continues in this vein proffering what he believes to be the considered fatherly advice of an internationally revered business grandee and knight of the realm to the up and coming generation of young local business people who, after all, have paid extravagantly for the privilege of listening to him.

Exactly ten minutes after the first word was spoken, he finishes with his last. He remains standing, acknowledging the applause resounding around the feasting hall, and revels in the glances of appreciation being sent in his direction. Eventually, giving a nod of acknowledgement to his appreciative audience, he sits down, pours himself a large glass of burgundy, and quaffs it down in one long draw whilst the honourable lady mayor pats him on the back by way of congratulation.

Five minutes after the coffee and brandy has been served, he senses the presence of someone settling down in the chair reserved for the chief executive. He turns around to see a smart young lady in a well tailored business suit. In the shock of seeing the chair occupied he doesn't immediately recognise the occupant.

"Well, what do you want?" he asks gruffly.

"Daddy - I just wanted to say thank you for your fantastic speech, it was what was needed tonight, though I do wish you could have acknowledged the chief executive as your daughter instead of referring to me as a he. I suppose you just did it to make me try harder when I work the room and have to explain, yet again, who I am."

The lights of perception hiding within the confines of his forgetful mind slowly start switching themselves back on.

"Where the hell were you when I was speaking? As the chief executive you are supposed to sit next to me – it's protocol you know."

"Daddy," she elongates the expression of the word in a humorous tone with an uplift of inflection on the 'y'. "You know exactly where I was, and it is too late in the day to get jealous. I was sat at the far end of the table, below the salt with mummy. Don't you remember? I asked you to invite her and you agreed. You know - I sometimes worry about your memory. Anyway, it would be polite if at least you would occasionally remove yourself from your exalted heights at the top of the table and visit the lesser minions at the lower half. You know - it's called networking. Anyway you could find it within that callous old business heart of yours to come and say hello to mum - you know, the mother of your children."

*******************************************

It is a month later as he sits at the head of the table situated within the building he likes to think of as his feasting hall, five minutes prior to delivering his speech, he momentarily forgets the name of the charity. He is the patron of several, and due to the similarity of their particular aims and objectives, and his increasing age, he sometimes suffers an understandable degree of amnesia regarding the specific details in the speech he is required to make.

The momentary lapse in concentration annoys him as it is a matter of immense personal pride he can speak to an audience without notes. This is not due to any particular improvisational skills (although some are obviously involved); it's just that he has, through the dedication of many hours practice, learnt by heart the key themes and structure of his 'charity 'speeches. He only has to fill in the missing elements of his address from information regarding the charity's recent good works and social successes. These particulars are derived from the data supplied to him on the day by the relevant incumbent chief executive. This additional knowledge is normally basic enough to be learnt and held securely within his once impeccably efficient short term memory on the actual day. He then uses the face of the chief executive as a mnemonic anchor to remember who and what he is talking about.

He turns around to see who is residing in the seat reserved for a person of such an august position. He sees the small man with weak eyes and dodgy teeth and thinks to himself - oh yes, it's that charity.

# Chapter 9 – The Councillor

'Where people come together
watch for the ruler who is silent
the one who is invisible to the naked eye'

As the Southern City Regional Area Planning Committee meeting moves inexorably into its second hour the councillor sighs, leans her left elbow to the right hand side of the table microphone, and places her weary head in her hand. She is well and truly bored.

Unless you are one, no-one really knows what it is like to be a local politician – especially one like this councillor who was accidentally persuaded to take on the role some fifteen years ago. She was approached to stand for election by a political friend she knew, and, after a little thought, she decided to give it a go - at the grand old age of fifty-one there was nothing to lose and anyway she needed a hobby having been forced into an early retirement from the local library, where, following the birth of her twins, she had earned a living for twenty years - local politics could be fun.

By the time of the election she had been residing within the city for over thirty five years and she instinctively knew, with a certain degree of personal conviction, that she had a great deal to give back to the community. The ward she would go on to represent was newly created from changes proposed by the Boundary Commission following the establishment of the new local unitary authority which replaced the historic city council, regional district councils and county council. She had a personal axe to grind - it was the new unitary authority that had effectively made her redundant before her time.

Shortly after its inauguration she was informed by the faceless directorate of the recently created department for local amenities her services were no longer required. She could, if she liked, apply for one of the new lesser paid roles within the service, however, they advised, it was probably in her better interests to take early retirement. So she left without receiving even the courtesy of a thank you for all her years of loyal and continuous service. She likes to think that during the intervening years as a local politician she has given those faceless officers more grief than they ever gave her.

Even back then her husband bored her as much as she bored him and so when the local party, struggling to find a suitable volunteer, asked her out of the blue to represent them in a ward she had absolutely had no chance of winning, she was excited at the prospect of getting away from him for a while - even if it was only for the duration of the election.

On election night, much to the shock of the local party, she wins the ward. This stunning victory generates considerable resentment towards her from the local party leader. He had rejected the opportunity to stand for her seat on the grounds it was obviously un-winnable - he was known, and is still known, for being a bad loser. It was, therefore, probably unfortunate when, during that particular election, he managed to lose the safe seat he had identified and insisted on standing for. His bitterness lingers to this very day and can be smelt lingering in the air with the putrid stench of a decomposing rat and observed hiding within the scowl on his face every time he has to address her. This occurs more frequently than he would care for - he was eventually re-elected to the council and now serves as chairman for the Southern City Regional Area Planning Committee - she has successfully held onto her seat ever since her initial election and considers it a duty to sit on this particular important committee.

From the moment of her first selection right up until today's meeting she has been fully engaged in her role as champion to the ward she represents in the south of the city, and, much to the annoyance of the council's executive, she expresses her personal views on each and every administrative, political and social issue on behalf of her local residents on what seems to be a daily basis. These interventions may not necessarily represent the actual views of the residents but as she keeps on being re-elected to the council, (albeit with a turnout of only 22% at the last election), she doesn't feel any urge or desire to take into account opinions differing to her own, because, as she correctly informs them, they can vote her out in four years time. This is, of course, if they can be bothered to make the journey from their respective households to the polling station. You see the councillor knows what is right and necessary for her ward, and for the city it is part of - she also knows what is wrong and inappropriate for her ward, and the city it is part of - especially when it comes to issues regarding urban regeneration. She has a long term plan for the area and slowly, with the subtle pace of a snail, she is achieving it.

But today she is bored – there are four contentious applications to be heard within this one meeting. She has just had to endure the pitiful whining of the general public, a regular ritual of all local planning committee meetings. This occurred during agenda item 5, the point in the proceedings where the local proles get a three minute slot to express their views about whatever it is that concerns them with the plans submitted for consideration. She wonders why it is only the incoherent members of society who choose to speak their unconstructed thoughts and unsolicited opinions at these meetings. They can barely keep on the subject matter in hand – surely they don't believe that by allowing a small industrial unit to be built next to the community hospital the council is planning to close the hospital and turn it into a business park? Two unrelated issues joined together with a conspiracy theory. Anyway they are now on agenda item 7a which just happens to be the application for the erection of the aforesaid industrial unit on land adjacent to the community hospital. The incessant debate has gone on interminably, and quite frankly this is not an application which remotely interests her even though her party has decided to oppose it to appease their potential voters.

"May I enquire as to whether madam councillor is awake?" her brain jolts to attention as she realises the chairman is addressing her.

In spite of the sudden shock to her system - for she has indeed drifted off - she manages to maintain the physical position she recently adopted, with her head in the palm of her hand, so as to give the impression she has chosen this particular posture intentionally. She turns her hand ever so slightly, moving the head a couple of inches to her left so she can gaze at the chairman with, what she hopes is, the cynical, witty, and sardonic look that will support the acerbic comment she is just about to make.

"Well master chairman, I was just wondering when you were going to get a grip on these proceedings. We do all have homes to go to, though I must admit I am beginning to forget what mine looks like."

A giggle emanates from her colleagues which, within its suppressed silence, is distinctly audible throughout the committee room.

He gives her a look of disdain - "I am aware that matters in the part of the city we are currently discussing may be of no interest to madam councillor, but may I remind her that some of the electorate she represents in the north of her ward live in close proximity to the proposed development and, judging from what we heard earlier, they appear to have some fairly major concerns regarding it."

She removes her head from the palm of her hand and turns hers upper torso so she can glare at the chairman.

"Of course I am deeply interested," there is just the slightest hint of sarcasm in her voice. She pauses before continuing. "Everyone knows my views on this matter; everyone knows everyone else's 'views on this matter; and the simplest fact would appear to be nobody is going to change their view on this matter. Nevertheless it is obviously important for everyone to get their three minutes of fame, so please allow me to continue with my silent meditation whilst I wait for you to call the vote." She turns her gaze away from the chairman, sits upright, and closes her right fist so she can inspect the overall state of her nail varnish.

Blah, blah and bloody blah. She is bored with the politics, fed up with supporting her colleagues, fed up with having to toe a party line she doesn't agree with, fed up with the cynical innuendo surrounding this trade. Yet, somehow, the resemblance of power she has over others, the validation of existence she receives from the electorate (either positive or negative), the status the role brings with it, and the sense of importance from being one of the city's leading citizens, all gel together to provide the necessary stimulus and motivation to sit through the dull drag of a council committee meeting.

She looks quizzically at the other honourable members in attendance, peering at them as though finally seeing their true nature for the first time emerging in full focus from the shadows of her experience. They, along with herself, are currently seated around a large horseshoe shaped ash wooden meeting table in the mock Victorian oaken styled committee room number 1, sitting opposite the general public, who themselves are sat, theatre style, as witnesses observing some form of archaic grand inquisition.

She concludes her observations and returns to the ongoing inspection of her nail varnish, confirming within herself what she has known for a long time – she doesn't really like any of her colleagues - nothing to do with their party politics, it's just the pathos they bring to their superficial air of personally inflicted self-importance. Nevertheless they form part of the local collective group known as the 'council'. The 'council' serves the unique purpose of enabling each councillor, subject to certain standards and conditions, to justify their own existence, and to close ranks and support fellow colleagues should anyone have the audacity to question their modus operandi or their overall relevance towards the general maintenance of the local administrative system.

She pauses in her reverie as the chairman asks them to vote. Out of sheer bloody mindedness she approves the application for the erection of an industrial unit on land adjacent to the community hospital, as it goes against the party line and will intensely annoy some of her party colleagues. Only another two applications to go before she has the chance to proselytise on her favourite subject – the demolition of the Four Feathers Public House and erection of 10 two bedroom and 7 one bedroom residential apartments.

The Four Feathers Public House sits on the crossroads of two major roads, one providing access to the city centre, with the other, a dual carriageway, taking a pivotal role as part of the inner ring road. On this road, opposite the pub, there is a parade of five run down shops consisting of, an off license, a newsagent/grocery shop, a Chinese take away, a shop selling second hand furniture, a charity shop, and the mandatory unit always available for let.

The brewery which owns the Four Feathers has been trying to sell the building for the last fifteen years and, since then, has consistently refused to spend any money on its refurbishment. The building is an eyesore, shabby with peeling paint and weed infested car park. The current application has been made by the local housing association who currently has an option from the brewery to purchase the land - she opposes the proposal. Her personal view is that, once the pub has been demolished, the site should be used to build a metro style supermarket with only a little social housing on top. This would increase retail provision in the area and shove a firework up the backside of the existing retail businesses in the parade making them 'pull their bloody socks up'. Unfortunately the officers of the planning department and some of her own political colleagues disagree with her.

Nevertheless, she is truly convinced a nice little supermarket would aid economic re-generation and be popular with her electorate. Consequently she would prefer the pub to remain as a rundown community amenity until she gets what she wants. The application in front of the committee today is definitely not the development she wants. She has managed to get seven similar applications for the site thrown out during the last ten years. She is not going to back down now, even though no commercial property developer appears to be interested in developing the site in the way she would prefer.

She pauses to vote on agenda item 7b - this time in line with the party whip. Only one more to go before agenda item 7d hits the floor with a resounding thump. She sighs again, causing her colleagues to look at her sharply. They have now been sitting in committee room 1 for over two and a half hours. She notices the look from her colleagues, smiles sarcastically at them, and feigns a yawn - the meeting is beginning to take on the sensation of a drug induced state of eternal recurrence with time and events turning around each other in an everlasting dance of dull repetition.

The councillor is a tall women, though not as tall as she once was. The passage of time has expressed its inevitable nature within the form of an osteoporosis which developed as a result of the hormonal change brought about by the onset of menopause. She has an imposing presence and a sophistication in purpose. Her figure is finely balanced. She is variously described as handsome, astute, severe, bad tempered or rude, the verdict depending on the observers current relationship with her. Regardless of her evolving age she still retains the striking dark red hair she has possessed for the last twenty years - she decided to colour in this way when her natural light auburn state transmogrified towards an ever increasing shade of grey. The new colour, she decided, represented and revealed the true nature of her fighting spirit and indomitable determination.

At the moment she is more than aware that the members of the public who have just spoken in support of agenda item 7d – The Demolition of the Four Feathers Public House and the erection of 10 two bedroom and 7 one bedroom residential apartments on the site, will consider her to be a complete and utter bitch for the way in which she has just dissed their political right to have a point of view. They had spouted nothing but banal nonsense. She only just managed not to laugh out loud while they were speaking. Any way she put them in their place. It's always the same when new people move into an area, they think they know what's best for the city regardless of the fact they don't know the traditions or the geopolitical nature of the district. Politics is politics and if you don't want to get burnt stay away from the fire; and, in relation to this particular application, she is the fire. OK, so they may think they have a worthwhile point of view but they should recognise she is also representing the majority of people who don't have one and who therefore, by default, agree with what she is doing.

Through the course of one's actuality within this wonderful planet, each individual human will be required to make choices concerning the way in which they conduct the orchestration of their being - decisions they believe will impact on the quality and fulfilment of their existence. It does not matter from which strata of human allegiance you belong or aspire to, you will have to face such choices, sometimes on a daily basis. How your decision is determined will be based on the values and beliefs created by your various upbringings and the nature of time within your creation. These key life changing decisions, including those involving the most intimate interaction with your nearest and dearest peers, will almost certainly pose the question which, for the most time, remains ignored in a present moment, especially in the one instant when the decision is required.

The question is simply this: Whilst fighting for what I consider to be right and true, in my endeavour for success in attaining this goal, will I behave in a way which undermines the basic integrity, rights, values and beliefs of another human being?

For the majority of humans, regardless of their intimacy with the underlying nature of this question, the answer, at least on the sub-conscious and reactive level, will be a unequivocal 'yes'. The problem for the councillor and her colleagues is they have answered 'no 'to this question so many times they have lost the sense of their own reality. Consequently they will always fail to see the illogical outcome and the irony of their behaviour when conversing in debate with each other, and with any lesser mortals who have opinions other than their own.

Anyway, the reduction of the Four Feathers into a heap of removable hardcore, and its replacement with residential apartments is not a case yet set in concrete. As in all such debates the economic arguments for and against are half for one and half for the other. Unfortunately with a political system whose approach to conflict resolution is based on the idea of competition, a third approach arising from the friction of the opposites is unlikely to see the dawn of day. Therefore you are either 'for' the development and opposed to the councillor, or 'against' the development and in accord with the councillor. There is no fourth way – in her opinion that would be prevarication and a waste of council tax payers 'money.

The arguments for and against the development can be summed up in a couple of sentences. Yes, the development will bring a much needed economic stimulus to an area in need of regeneration. No, the development will not bring about a much needed economic stimulus to an area in need of regeneration - a different type of development is needed and we are happy to wait and carry on supporting the Four Feathers as a much needed local amenity. Of course none of the councillors supporting the latter argument would ever allow themselves to be seen frequenting the Four Feathers hallowed environs or treading on its cigarette burnt, beer stained, once colourful striped orange carpet - most certainly not, they are far too delicate - such patronage will be left for the lesser salubrious to undertake. Anyway - much to the annoyance of the councillor, the planning officers have recommended the application be approved on the grounds it fulfils the requirements of the city's core planning strategy, policies 1 and 2. Well sod them! She is going to fight.

Two hours and forty three minutes into the Southern City Regional Area Planning Committee meeting is probably not the best time for a deep philosophical question to suddenly erupt into the forefront of the councillor's neocortex. To be quite fair to the question, however, it had been rumbling about within the deeper recesses of her limbic system for some time trying to make itself heard. Finally it succeeded - five and a half minutes following the commencement of the soon to be interminable discussions regarding the application listed as agenda item 7c – Renovation of Barn into a Visitor Centre situated at The Rising Sign Vineyard, Village Lane, The Village.

By some quirk of fate resulting from the development of a large housing estate, which virtually connects The Village to the City, together with subsequent changes to the parish boundaries, this particular application falls under the jurisdiction of the Southern City Regional Area Planning Committee. The fractious debate which has arisen enables councillors for and against the proposed development to practice the art of political sparring, where the winner is decided by the number of 'so there' points scored against their opponent.

This debate is about whether the access road to The Rising Sign Vineyard can cope with the additional twenty or so cars each week ferrying visitors wishing to discover more about the ancient art of British wine production. It appears the vineyard's neighbours are 'disgusted 'and 'outraged 'that they are going to be subjected to a mass immigration of visitors who are not of the village. As the rural councillor representing the ward covering The Village explains, this is what happens when you allow a city person, who does not understand the ways of The Village, to invade and take over a run-down non-economic dilapidated farm, renovate it, plant a vineyard, and turn it into a profitable business venture. Why can't people just mind their own business, respect the past, and allow everything to stay the way it has always been.

The debate slowly turns into the well rehearsed game known as 'City v Rural'. Councillors representing rural wards accuse the councillors representing the city wards of not understanding the ways of country folk, being only interested in the city and divesting all funds which should be invested within outlying villages toward the aforesaid city. City councillors smirk at the ignorance of their peasant colleagues and accuse them of living in an idyllic dream of a past that never existed. During today's argument they raise a great many other matters which, quite frankly, bear scant relevance to the actual planning application in question. Egos get damaged and bruised necessitating the soothing ointment of an apology for a variety of imagined misdemeanours from both sides, enabling all the aggrieved parties to make the requisite victory speech accepting each other's apology.

So it is at exactly five forty three in the evening, as the crescendo point of the debate over agenda item 7c – Renovation of Barn into a Visitor Centre situated at The Rising Sign Vineyard, Village Lane, The Village, slowly reaches upward toward its zenith, when years of suppressed annoyance over the behaviour of her colleagues, the endless rounds of canvassing where the majority of residents she met couldn't give a toss, and the endless whingeing of the few who did, finally resulted in the emergence of a question which demanded to be seen and acknowledged. It took a number of forms in order to achieve its aim, namely; ' —What the fuck am I doing here?' -' Is this really what my life has come to? '- 'What am I doing living in this miserable city surrounded by miserable people with a miserable husband who, quite frankly, doesn't give a shit about anything I do?'

She can no longer see any point to the role she is inhabiting. The political reality behind her job is merely to provide a firewall preventing the general public from attaining access to the people who actually make the decisions – i.e. those faceless local government officers, like the ones who made her 'redundant', and the two currently sitting next to the chairman who have recommended for approval agenda item 7d – The Demolition of the Four Feathers Public House and the erection of 10 two bedroom and 7 one bedroom residential apartments.

At precisely six o clock the chairman calls for a vote and, in line with the other 'city' councillors, she votes for agenda item 7c – Renovation of Barn into a Visitor Centre situated at The Rising Sign Vineyard, Village Lane, The Village. The application is approved by the majority of the committee, accompanied by the snorts of derision and indignation from the 'rural' councillors who, of course, voted against.

When the chairman has settled everyone down he introduces agenda item 7d.

"So turning to agenda item 7d – The Demolition of the Four Feathers Public House and the erection of 10 two bedroom and 7 one bedroom residential apartments. Our planning officers have recommended we approve the application and have advised there are no substantive or material reasons for refusing it. It complies with the council's core development strategy - in particular by promoting economic regeneration for an impoverished part of the city, whilst, at the same time, increasing the stock of affordable housing in the area. However, I know this is a contentious application and there are some amongst us, well one in particular, who would like to see this application refused."

He looks toward the councillor, and continues,

"Madam councillor, you requested to speak against this application at the start of the meeting – I hand the floor over to you."

She looks over to the chairman and presses the engagement button on her table microphone. It stutters into life, creating a slightly odd echo which audibly resonates an emptiness throughout committee room 1, expectantly awaiting to be fulfilled. She looks at her notes, picks them up and folds them, places them back on the table, picks up her hand bag from the floor, and places the papers within its confines. She looks back over to the chairman who is observing her impatiently. The silent echo expands, expressing its own impatience with the ongoing silence. The eternity of a couple of seconds is suddenly terminated - she speaks

"I have decided to withdraw my objections; I have nothing to say on this matter".

The shock wave is palpable. Her colleagues cannot believe the words emanating from the councillors mouth. They look at her in silence waiting for her to continue - surely it is a joke? She remains silent.

"I am not sure I heard you correctly – do you mind repeating that?" The chairman looks at her in surprise.

"I do mind repeating myself, however, as you apparently failed to hear me, what I said was - 'I have decided to withdraw my objections'; I have nothing further to say in this matter." The tone of her voice carries its normal acerbic temperament and yet is also tinged with a certain uncharacteristic degree of resignation.

"I have to say I am somewhat surprised. You have made your feelings extremely apparent to the members of the public who supported this application earlier and I am aware you have led our planning officers a merry little dance over the years with similar applications for the site in question. Do you not feel you owe us an explanation for this rather surprising volte-face?" The chairman looks at her in askance.

For a moment she feels self-conscious. She is aware of being a centre of attention and, in the overall scheme of her life, this would not have normally bothered her, except this evening she suddenly feels confused, lost, and lacking purpose. She looks at the chairman, and suddenly experiencing a massive lack of confidence, looks away from his gaze and turns her eyes downwards to the floor.

"No I will not explain my reasons, master chairman, and I don't believe there are any particular standing orders requiring me to do so."

The chairman stares at her - the room remains silent. Within the surrounding silence a member of the public coughs. The sound is enough to re-animate the Southern City Regional Area Planning Committee Meeting. The chairman looks away from the lady councillor, glances at the papers in front of him, consults with the planning officers sat on either side of him, looks at the wrist watch on his right arm, and speaks.

"In the absence of madam councillor wishing to share her views with us would any of the other fellow members care to speak against this planning application?"

Nobody volunteers to speak - in all fairness they are completely stunned and whilst it is highly probable that the lady councillor, through the sheer strength of her personality, would have convinced at least a few of her colleagues to vote against the proposal, in the absence of her one line whip the plans for the the Demolition of the Four Feathers Public House and the erection of 10 two bedroom and 7 one bedroom residential apartments are approved unanimously with one abstention.

*********************************************************

As the Southern City Regional Area Planning Committee meeting moved inexorably into its third hour to deal with the final item on the agenda; item 8 - urgent items, the councillor sighs, leans her left elbow to the right hand side of the table microphone, and places her weary head in her hand. She is well and truly bored.

# Part 4 - Managing the Vine

'It is only through hard work that the rewards of life arrive
Work and you will succeed
Work and you will be recognised
Work and you will show your worth to all around you'

To achieve any form of consideration toward the management of the vine, you will need to understand your relationship with it. Of course, not many people will choose to confess an affinity with the vine even if they are aware of it - why would they when there is so much at stake in their everyday association with the society they depend upon for existence.

Over the aeons we have had much time to reflect on the questions posed by the existence of the vine and we are repeatedly drawn back to one specific line of inquiry - can humanity cultivate and manage an open and healthy relationship with it - one which would be conducive to their overall well-being?

It is apparent the contagion associated with the vine multiplies most aggressively within the vicinity of those people who are susceptible to loneliness and present a degree of sadness in their bearing. Following a logical course of inquiry the answer to our question could appear to be relatively simple - happy individuals, who are not lonely, should be able to live harmoniously within the vicinity of the vine.

Happiness, of course, is a subjective concept, measurable only by the individual in terms of the sadness they have already experienced in life. Naturally if they have already experienced sadness, they must also have already created the appropriate environment in which the vine would thrive.

Nevertheless, we asked ourself, would the risk of contagion be ameliorated if potential victims were in a romantic and loving relationship with another of their species? Surely it is within all such relationships where human beings are at their most satiated?

Alas, it would appear not. Whilst many people feel instinctively, when engaged in a relationship with the one 'special' person they have momentarily found themselves to be with, that absolutely nothing will impact upon their ecstatic happiness; it would appear, such periods of 'contentedness' are generally short lived and last only long enough for each partner to appreciate that the other will not provide them with the personal validation they need in order to justify their existence in the world. When the gluttony of lust and attraction wears off most people feel the sense of loneliness and sadness that is symptomatic of the presence of the vine. Romantic attachments in general may actually encourage the contagion to infect your life.

We asked ourselves, would open exchanges of dialogue between those 'enlightened' beings who become aware of the vine ameliorate the fate of all mortals living within the contagion it brings?

Alas, we concluded it would not. When 'enlightened' individuals become aware of anything of substance and are prepared to enter into an open conversation regarding its nature with other cognoscenti, friends or therapists, they soon discover they disagree over the essential elements of its being. Very rarely is there anything fresh or renewing within the sound of their voices – there is little movement toward the discovery of anything new. Everything which could be said has already been told, and your societies' belief of becoming more civilised and creative is the illusion of progressive time and the naivety of history. Most of the time such 'enlightened' beings, regardless of gender and age, merely fling immutable emotive points of view at each other in the hope they validate their worth within the world – the rest of the time they serve up flaccid platitudes to provide each other with a deluded sense of warmth and comfort. In the stagnant environment of such dialogue the vine flourishes.

We also contemplated whether total solitude would protect an individual against the contagion brought through the existence of the vine. If total solitude were to exist then it may provide the answer. However, we simply observe solitude rarely exists in any substantive form on your planet. Loneliness, yes – solitude, no. Even within the most silent regions of your planet a person can't exist without the support of their 'society'. Can you have security outside 'society'? Could you survive for any length of time without what 'society' provides - food, shelter, warmth? In the past many of your species searched for solitude in order to escape from 'society' - they merely discovered the loneliness whose only desire is madness.

You might ask then whether or not your rulers - those politicians who command your daily subservience, having once recognised the truth of the vine, could manage its existence on behalf of humanity. We would ask you - which 'society' would these 'rulers' come from? From our own observations your rulers can only manage through the annihilation and assimilation of their neighbours - through war, genocide and rape.

We are still searching for the answer - this is why we are telling you these little stories. However, what we can advise you is your relationship to the vine is personal. The only way to control its hold over your life is through dedication to hard work; your individual attention to responsibility; and the way in which you choose to honour and undertake the duties of your living.

\*\*\*\*\*\*\*\*\*\*\*\*\*\*\*\*\*\*\*\*\*\*\*\*\*\*\*\*\*\*\*

# Chapter 10 – The Pastor

'It is only in the absence of dialogue
that truth is found
So hide from the noise of your chatter
for in silence there may be safety'

The pastor walks from the vestry situated within the north transept, towards the Chapel of the Lady situated within the south transept, stopping briefly at the chancel arch to bow respectfully before the lime stone altar table and the cross residing below the east end windows. When he arrives at the entrance for the worship area designated to the Lady, he pauses - sighs - and steps over the threshold into the chapel. He chooses a pew on the left hand side, three rows down from the ash wood altar prayer table - sits down, places his hands on his knees, finds sensation in his feet, closes his eyes, becomes aware of his breathing, and begins to recite his Kyrie Eleison. Thus begins the full half hour prayer meditation he has faithfully undertaken at 6.30 am every morning, in precisely the same way, in exactly the selfsame spot, for the last twenty three years of his life as pastor in residence of the Church of Universal Values.

The Church of Universal Values was founded in 1886 by the first pastor, the renowned Christian Philosopher and Thinker on his return from a sabbatical mission to explore the foundation of Christian culture on the Indian subcontinent. It was during these travels he was inspired to deeper faith through the example of a yogic master he met in an Ashram situated in the foothills of the Himalayas on the bank of the river Ganges. Finding a deeper inspiration towards esoteric life he remained at the ashram as a resident pupil for the following ten years. He then returned to the country of his birth to fulfil a hefty schedule of public speaking, arranged and organised by the internationally regarded publishers of his somewhat extensive travelogue.

It was during this literary tour he discovered that his universal fame had put him at odds with the ecclesiastical hierarchy who could not find it within their hearts to provide him with a parish suitable for his ego. His devotees, however, were of the wealthy variety and eager to learn the unique secrets and insights he had uncovered in his quest for the foundations of inspirational worship  - for it was claimed he had uncovered much during his studies in India. With the moneys left to him by a friendly widow, a foundation was established from which the independent church of no official denomination was built, raised on the virtues of philosophy, creativity, service and work. From then on and unto this day the Church of Universal Values likes to think of itself as being at the forefront of Christian esoteric thought. The reality is, that with the passage of time, the renowned Christian Philosopher and Thinker has largely been forgotten and the church is barely recognised or known outside the confines of its own congregation and the somewhat over populated city in which it was founded.

Today the pastor will officiate at his final Sunday morning service for the Church of Universal Values where, as we alluded earlier, he has been the caretaker of lost souls for the last twenty three years. Generally twenty three years in one ecclesiastical post would, certainly nowadays, be considered somewhat rare – either a sign of total devotion by one person to their flock, or, more likely, a lack of desire for growth in both career and personal development. However, it is not uncommon within the history of the Church of Universal Values who, within its history, has only commissioned three pastors since the original founder walked through the entrance of the building erected for his life's work. The shortest recorded term held in this sacerdotal role, prior to the existing holder, was the original pastor's successor, his son, who remained on duty for thirty five years from 1920 to 1955. Once they were appointed, incumbents, in a similar fashion to the monarchy, were expected to remain in post and 'on the job' until they died. Therefore, to all intents and purposes, he has been made redundant - asked politely to retire by the church elders who run the church on behalf of the congregation who own it and therefore employ him. They want him 'out of the way' because they feel he no longer projects an image appropriate to the direction in which the church now wishes to rebrand itself.

During the last five years the balance of authority and power coexisting between himself and the elders have shifted somewhat significantly in favour of the latter. On his appointment it was presumed he would continue with tradition - take up the mantle of his predecessor as protector of the unique truths preserved within the fabric of the Church's culture and reveal these truths to generation upon generation of the congregation as part of his ongoing ministry up until the moment of his death. Prior to his impending departure from the mortal plane, a successor would be identified, trained and mentored for the forthcoming vacancy. He would remain in authority until his final breath had been taken.

Now he is being released before his allotted time and although he is beyond what would normally be considered a natural age for retirement, he can't quite comprehend why or how an officially ordained minister, a universal seeker of the mystical union with the universal father, is supposed to retire from his life's work.

The pastor had always been suspicious of ill-informed philosophical debate regarding the nature of spirituality, especially those conducted between the uneducated and the ill-informed. He became especially concerned when such discourses started making their unsolicited presence felt within the domestic weekly meetings held to organise the day to day administrative management of the church, the maintenance of its fabric, and, congregational worship. It was that final agenda item of the meetings (congregational worship) which provided the excuse. The intention behind its original inclusion was purely to confirm who was going to do what and when within the weekly services; i.e., undertake the readings; perform the intercessions; act as sacristan, and help serve the lord's supper. Instead he had been forced to endure endless discussions where the lesser un-ordained in the truth would exhaustively ponder over some aspect of god and his son – for example, does god grow older as we grow older? - does god change as we change? - does god have regrets?

Regardless of his attempts to curb such immature spiritual behaviour they persisted. Eventually he gave up and removed himself from their seemingly pointless discussions on the pretext of attending to outstanding pastoral care duties. He was disappointed by their behaviour and made his feelings known. He saw within their interminable gossip a form of escapism from direct experience - an excuse not to 'do' or engage with the invisible living quality the church could provide them with. Instead they were creating a god in their own image and conceiving a new line of 'exterior truth'. He was equally disturbed when they started to disseminate their discourses amongst the congregation through the minutes of their meetings - these were written up at the end of each month, bound up into a pamphlet and published quarterly under the title 'The Truth from Beyond'. It was now even being made available to non-attending church members for a monthly subscription fee through the new website.

The Victorian church is constructed to a cruciform design in dark red brick. The interior retains the natural colour of the exterior brick and there is little ornamentation except for the spring vines stretching from floor to ceiling painted carefully onto each and every pillar. There are 16 of these columns set out in four rows of four creating and maintaining the structure of the nave, the ceiling and transepts. The floor is laid out with an even darker red glazed pan tile. All this is offset by the simple plain ash wood used in the construction of the pews lining the nave, the choir stalls, lectern and organ casing.

The windows are set quite high, close to the vaulted ceilings, and glazed in a pale bottle green glass. The light from the windows together with the spring vines on the pillars exude a pale green shimmer within the red brick so when you first enter the church it feels as though you are walking through a forest in the mist of an early morning dawn. The lime stone altar table, which is never adorned with a cloth, is positioned under the east end window in a way that catches the light. This gives off an otherworldly glow which can be perceived and sensed from any spot within the building. Hanging from the ceiling, just above the altar, is an ornate cross carved from black granite. It rests on a backing of cream Italian marble shaped in the form of a six pointed star made from six connecting lines partially enclosed within a silver circle. Underneath the cross is a solitary candle which is always lit whenever any person is present within the building.

In his understanding of the world, the church had laid its foundations to protect the flock from the contamination of societal living - and from from all he sees and hears his inevitable conclusion is that society is indeed befouled and there is absolutely nothing to be gained from engaging with it. Why the elders and congregation couldn't feel satisfied and sustained from the gift of prayer and meditation freely available within the sanctuary of the church he did not know. Why had they fallen into the trap of wishfully believing they could save the saveless? How could they believe it was incumbent on them to save the souls of others before they had redeemed their own? If it had been the intention of the church to engage within society the founding pastor and his congregation wouldn't have built a church but rather a community centre with an open for all sign on the door.

Surely they didn't really believe they should stray outside their place of worship and subject themselves under the scrutiny of the uninitiated? It makes no sense whatsoever - the ordinary daily existence of society is far too messy, dirty and corrupt. Engagement with the everyday ordinary would taint the purity of the rarefied and mystical atmosphere he and his predecessors had so carefully cultivated on behalf of the congregation. The duty of this church was to pray for the poor, pray for the correct guidance of the world's rulers, and steadfastly ignore the squalor and pollution which the locals have to suffer on a daily basis - 'do not engage with the homeless on the street, come to church and pray for their souls'.

Yet now for some reason or other the elders want to leave the sanctuary of the church and identify with society. They want to become 'charismatic 'and 'evangelical'. They want to sell the internal truths of the

Church of Universal Values outside the very confines of the building which was built to keep them safe and protected whilst also maintaining the independent environmental conditions necessary for effecting mystical union with the universal creator of everything.

He has tried to reason with them – people come to the truth, truth does not go out to the people. Truth is a limited commodity and there is not enough of it to feed everyone. Not all are chosen to be saved. It is not the role of this church to convert the eternal atheists on to a path of truth too narrow for them to navigate. His role, quite simply, is to be educator to the converted - I.e. those people who, by some quirk of fate, have happened to walk through the north transept doors of the Church of Universal Values, and chosen to stay.

He didn't understand the logic of the elders 'arguments, partly, he suspected, because there wasn't any logic to be found. Their primary premise was the church should be an integral part of society and fight for justice and the overthrow of poverty, sickness and disease. They were so wrong. There will always be poverty, sickness and disease. There will always be corruption and politics. The role of the church is to provide room to escape the clutches of societal misdeeds and recuperate from its excesses in the bliss brought on through the knowledge that within these sanctified walls it is possible to move above such mundanity and seek divine union.

The radical conception which arrived somewhat lazily into the elders thought processes was that they were privy to a way of living life capable of reducing the stress and hardship associated with an individual's daily experience of having to engage within society in order to achieve the income associated with sustained planetary existence. Why should this delectable titbit of truth remain a secret when it could be packaged up in neat little parcels and marketed to the world at large? The cost they placed on this teaching would deter the less serious seekers, increase the congregation, and refurbish the coffers enabling the church to extend its ministry ever further. He could not agree with their decision to sell off, what was to his own mind, the church's gold and silver, and turn it into a commodity available only to those with the money to squander on their own personal development. They in their turn decided they needed a more charismatic and evangelical pastor amenable to their wishes, choices and desires.

This Sunday morning, like the majority of Sunday mornings before, he has arisen from his sleeping at approximately 6.00 am, washed, shaved, dressed, gone into the kitchen, boiled the kettle, made a pot of tea, poured himself one cup with a little milk, drank it, walked across from the manse to the church building, unlocked the door, lit the candle on the altar underneath the cross, said a short prayer, returned to the north transept vestry, filled the tea urn with water and set it to boil, crossed over from the north transept to the south transept, stopping halfway to bow to the cross and altar, and then entered the Chapel of the Lady for his half an hour of prayer meditation. After this period of prayer he readies himself to lead the Sunday morning worship. And, as already mentioned, having ministered to his flock faithfully for twenty three years, today will be the last time he ever leads the Sunday service to this particular congregation. As from approximately 12.30 pm, after the final cup of tea or coffee has been drunk, he will become an outcast to this church, and although fondly remembered, never welcome within its precincts ever again. For once a minister has left a church, the church truly leaves the minister and continues with its own life, as one divorced and taken with a new lover.

On Monday morning the removal firm will come and empty the manse of the few belongings he has and transport them to the bungalow he has rented on the edge of a village some significant distance away from the city. At the end of today's service he will be driven by taxi to his new abode and once there continue his life in a way he cannot even begin to comprehend. For you see twenty three years serving his god and congregation is a long time to develop habitual ways of living which, although appropriate and spirit enhancing within the security of the church, are not necessarily life affirming outside its sanctuary. Financially there is no problem. He will not be struggling to find funds in order to maintain his continuing existence. He has invested in a pension and has a tidy sum put away in a variety of different saving schemes. Although he has never received much of a salary his outgoings were low. He had been given the manse rent free to live in and most of his household expenses were paid for by the church. He wasn't, never had been, and never will be married. He does not drink of the vine and is a vegetarian happily growing most of his own food in the manse garden when not working on church matters.

He first started attending the Church of Universal Values in his early twenties after leaving the city university with a degree in ethical philosophy. He had developed an interest in comparative theologies and came across the church whilst undertaking a personal research project on the ethical variances between conformist and non-conformist religious traditions. He was taken with the theological stance represented through its liturgy, joined and shortly afterwards found himself being mentored by the then pastor, who he eventually succeeded. The church elders of those days were particularly keen to ensure the succession from one pastor to another stayed well within the confines of the church and keep it, so to say, within the existing church family. After showing a keen interest in theological practicalities, and also having failed to get any form of employment which needed his particular brand of knowledge, he was encouraged to enter the reputable Anglican Independent Theological College with the aim of becoming recognised as an 'officially' ordained minister of religion. The elders of the church agreed to pay all fees and expenses - they felt it was important for their potential replacement as pastor to receive his commission within the line of tradition from Saint Peter.

He was ordained, returned as apprentice to the pastor, and was inducted to the ministerial office when the incumbent finally died twenty three years ago. Since the day of his inauguration his life has followed the same daily, weekly and yearly routine following the church's own unique liturgical calendar. His role is simply to investigate, to meditate, to write, to pray, to feed his flock and lead them in their universal search for truth.

The first four items on this 'to do 'list require four days of input during the week and the remaining two require three days. From Monday to Saturday he opens the church to the congregation at 7.30 am in the morning and 6.00 pm in the evening for one hour of shared prayer and meditation. Every Sunday he leads morning worship at 10.30 am, and evening prayer at 6.00 pm. Tonight, however, he will not be leading evening prayer. This morning's worship, as previously mentioned, is the last service, a final opportunity for his flock to pray for him, say farewell, and, speed him on his way.

He remembers with great fondness the elders who appointed him. Regrettably, those who had nurtured and cared for him all those years ago are now long gone. It is a new generation of 'elders' who, along with the membership, own the church today. The oldest 'elder 'is forty years of age. The pastor is now the oldest surviving member of the congregation from the days of his appointment. He can't quite recall when it happened, but all of a sudden, over a space of five to six years, the elderly membership dropped off. Many had just simply died, but others stopped attending. A younger congregation evolved into the body of the church.

As a result the Church of Universal Values had a sudden surge in popularity because its quasi mystical outlook suited the fashionistas of the time. In fact a young couple, celebrities in their own field of personal development, started attending with some of their friends. They had taken a keen interest in the teachings and in the space of six months got heavily involved in the daily running of the church. He had thought they were the future and yet they suddenly stopped attending as quickly as they had first got involved. At the time they had been busy setting up some sort of psychotherapeutic personal development programme. With hindsight he couldn't help thinking that a great many of the church's problems had only arisen as a result of their involvement, as if something poisonous had inveigled its way into the sub-structure of the building.

He slowly raises himself from the chair, crosses himself and walks back through the door of the Chapel of the Lady into the south transept. He walks across through the centre of the church briefly stopping to bow respectfully toward the cross and altar before returning to the vestry in the north transept. There he checks the urn and turns the temperature dial down. He goes to the wardrobe to select and organise the vestments he is going to wear for this final service. As he does this a thought suddenly breaks through the veil of his mind protecting the fabric of his own certainty and faith. The thought takes the shape of an existential question, a question which he has, surprisingly perhaps, never considered before. The thought simply asks " —what is the point of all and everything you have ever said or done?"

He suddenly feels faint as if all the blood has decided to depart from his brain to escape down towards his feet. To stop himself from falling he clutches onto the back of one of the old Victorian wooden chairs placed in the vestry for pre-service meditation and prayer. He pauses for a moment and then sits down. He contemplates his current situation and smiles to himself ruefully. "That's a pretty interesting question to turn up just now." Deciding to hold the question within his self he gets up and walks out of the vestry into the main body of the church where he starts preparing the theatre of worship. This generally consist of ensuring the church bible placed on the lectern (situated at the edge of the north transept) is open at the right place for the first reading; setting out his notes for the sermon on the pulpit (situated at the edge of the south transept); and re-arranging the celebrant and two side chairs (situated in front of the altar) by moving them ever so slightly by a few micro millimetres so their positioning is more pleasant to his sight.

At 9.30 am the musician walks in, and, as always, makes some derisory comment about the music selection for the service. As the musician moves over to the organ he comments he will miss the pastor but guesses the pastor must be pretty relieved to be finally retiring after so many years. The pastor ignores the comments. He is more than aware no-one really understands the tradition of the Church with regard to the longevity of the incumbent pastors any longer. The musician powers up the organ and starts improvising the rather predictable Celtic meanderings that appear to be his one and only creative forte. A few minutes later the church secretary walks in clutching a vase full of flowers which she places on a ledge in front of the pulpit. She says good morning to the pastor but appears somewhat embarrassed and can't quite make eye contact with him.

At 10.00 am the congregation start arriving. They file into their seats and the gentle murmur of conversation can be heard harmonising with the Celtic meanderings still being masticated on the organ by the musician. The pastor moves to the vestry and sits quietly in prayer and meditation. He is joined by the secretary and treasurer who enter quietly and take chairs opposite to his. They sit in silence for fifteen minutes when suddenly, with a silent accord, they get up. The treasurer leaves the vestry first, followed by the secretary; the pastor takes up the rear. They walk in a silent procession to the main body of the church where the congregation is waiting for the morning service to start. As they enter the nave the congregation stands. The treasurer bows to the altar and takes the side seat to the right of the celebrants chair. The secretary moves to the lectern. The pastor bows to the altar and takes his seat. The organ rises to a crescendo and concludes on a final chord indicating the start of proceedings. The congregation falls silent. The secretary speaks.

"Good morning to you all, and especially to you who are visiting us today. It so good to see so many of you. As most of you are aware this morning's service will be the final one led by our pastor prior to his retirement. It is an opportunity for us to wish him well for this new stage in his life and offer our prayers and thanksgiving for his selfless service to us, his flock, for the last twenty three years. If I am right in thinking he has worshipped at this church for over thirty five years. He has seen many changes and has led us to our current position, a place where we are much stronger as a community than we have ever been before. It is now only right that he now takes a rest and passes on the baton to a younger person. There will be no evening prayer tonight, however, there will be a church meeting open for members to discuss the future direction of the church and the appointment of a new pastor to lead us forward. If you are a member I would encourage you to come along." She pauses before continuing.

"After today's service we will be serving refreshments in the north transept." She concludes with a smile, steps away from the lectern, bows before the altar and takes the side seat to the left of the pastor. The pastor stands, moves down from the altar towards towards the centre of the church and his congregation. He looks around the expectant faces, pauses, smiles and then speaks.

"My dear friends today we reached the end of an era. We have been on a journey together and we have arrived at the crossroads where I will go in one direction and you will go in another. Today I was due to deliver my final sermon to you, my flock. This morning, in my meditation and prayer I realised it was no longer appropriate. Therefore there will be no sermon today. However, before I lead you in our final act of worship together there are a few things I need to say to you, thoughts which will raise questions which cannot necessarily be answered but nevertheless would benefit from reflection.

As I have said we are at the end of an era. I am the last in a line of pastors who have followed a tradition established by the church's founder. This tradition was transmitted orally from one pastor to the next over a significant apprenticeship. When I leave today the tradition will end. I do not know whether this will be a good or bad thing. The key to our tradition was that this church should provide its congregation with a haven where the individual can commune with god with a degree of ease not available within the hustle and bustle of society. The tradition of this church was to stand outside society and provide this blessing to its members. From today this will no longer be the case.

You should now question everything I have ever taught you. You should treat everything I have ever said with doubt and suspicion. My ministry to you was total and complete. If one part of it is lacking then the whole edifice collapses to the ground. Personally I have no alternative but to conclude part of it must have been lacking otherwise you would not have asked me to retire. I had no desire to leave you or this post which I have held for the last twenty three years.

So I have come to some conclusions which I would like to share with you. Firstly, whatever you think you are doing that is right, it is most probably wrong. Whatever you think is perfect in your life, it could probably be better. When you consider that you have a talent which others do not have, you are probably deluded. And, finally, however close you think you are to God, you will never be close enough. Let us stand and worship God.

# Part 5 - Living with the Vine

'One road is said to be true
But then so is another?
The answer to the conundrum depends upon the angle of
your perception
And in the twilight hours of your life much that is invisible
becomes clearer to the vision'

Do you feel we are deceiving you in anyway? It is not our intention to. We want you to enjoy and live your life on this earth as you perceive it. We did not see the vine until our loving mother revealed her secrets to us. We were so young at the time and didn't realise her intention. This was our mistake and one we have spent thousands of years trying to rectify on your behalf.

So what about love you may ask? Well we have to leave you to draw your own conclusions.

At this point on your journey there is not much more we can tell you - for the moment we will leave you with one final story.

# Chapter 11 – The Lover

*'You think you know me – you think you know who I am.
Until you know me and know the nature of sacrifice
You cannot judge or seek to know the dead'*

When he is awake his eyes appear to be focussed on an area where the white ceiling meets the upper wall, somewhere to the left of the door which provides access to this private room within the city hospital. When he is asleep we have no idea what his eyes are focussed on for they are residing deep within his soul as it awaits the final departure. The walls of the room are of the typical scuffed uniform white which hospital rooms of this nature tend to adopt - they are free from any form of decoration - there are no pictures or photographs to disturb the clinical sterility of the space. The only objects within the room are six plastic grey chairs, a bedside cabinet, and the various life monitors measuring the final countdown marking the end of his current existence in human form. On the bedside cabinet there is a picture of his only son and the two grandchildren.

On one of the plastic grey chairs there sits a lady – in her early seventies, dressed in a smart white blouse, light blue cardigan, and tweed grey trousers. She gives the impression of being tall, athletic, fit and healthy despite her advancing years. Her hair is brilliant white and falls elegantly onto her shoulders.

Quietly she holds his hand, very gently so that she is attuned to the slightest feeling of pressure he may still be able to apply through his fingers to acknowledge anything she might say. She has sat with him for a long time, long before he arrived at this hospital. However, for her at least, at this one moment time has stopped still. Today she arrived just after breakfast, went out at lunch to pick up her prescription painkillers from the chemist, and returned shortly after two pm. It is now three thirty and one of the helpers has just brought round the afternoon tea and biscuit.

"How are you today, and how is he?" she pours out the dark brown fluid from a large metal tea pot into a polystyrene cup, splashes in a little milk and hands it to the lady.

"Oh you know – surviving. Thank you for the tea. How are you?" she replies.

"Well you know, Graham, my second boy, the one married to Felicity, their youngest one, Bobby, started school yesterday. You should have seen him in his little uniform – he was so cute. He said to me – Nan, he said, I'm really looking forward to going to school today - I am - honest. He's a little rascal. He's going to break some hearts that one. Anyway, like I said the other day, my Jimmy is still having a tough time at work. We don't know if they are going to make him redundant or not. God alone knows what will happen if they do – we can't live off what I earn here."

She smiles sympathetically at the helper, takes the polystyrene cup in both hands, sips at the tea slowly and continues her lonely vigil, as she has done, faithfully, for the last fourteen days.

There is very little the specialists, nurses and doctors can say about his current state except explain the simple reality he is suffering from terminal closure. Finally all his major organs are giving out in a slow procession, moving away from the responsibility of maintaining life within his body.

She puts down her tea and picks up his hand again. It is cold so she places it, along with hers, under the quilt.

"Typical, let your hands get cold, I have told you about that so many times. It's a good job I'm here." She smiles to herself, she knows somewhere deep down in her being he can hear her - that he can feel her presence.

She gave her life to him some forty years ago. He was in an abusive relationship with an alcoholic. He had met his wife whilst at The Boarding School where during a period of teenage fumbling they had adventurously decided to experiment inserting his penis into her vagina. Unfortunately within the very few seconds it had taken for him to ejaculate, he failed to withdraw as promised. The unhappy result of their adventure led to her pregnancy, the removal of both boy and girl from the school, and, nine months later, the birth of their only son. It had also necessitated in his one and only marriage. The parents of the teenage adventurer were of a fundamentalist and devout religion who could neither condone an abortion, nor, a child born outside wedlock. The adventurer's female consort had a wealthy mother and step-father who simply wanted the troublesome girl out of their life.

However, both sets of parents were generous in nature and, on their children's behalf, took out a mortgage on a semi-detached house in the suburbs of the city. At the ripe old age of eighteen he had been married off to the sixteen year old and they moved into the house kitted out with all the old furniture the parents no longer wanted or needed. There they lived with their one and only child, supported, in the earliest years, by his parents until, he attained the professional qualifications required to call himself an accountant and got a job. The lady, currently at the side of the hospital bed, was his initial supervisor at the internationally recognised firm whose head offices just happened to be in the city where they both lived.

Their affair, like most affairs, was built on sexual innuendo and attraction. She couldn't remember who led who on, it had seemed organic in its naturalness. Eventually it resulted in her asking him to take her home one afternoon to collect some files accidentally left there, and inviting him in to the house for a drink. Somewhat predictably the drink turned into something more illicit in nature.

It is within the theatre of Eros that the key members of the cast hardly ever consider what they are doing as being immoral or wrong in anyway. Naturally, there is an instinctive sense of conscience resulting in the need to justify their own behaviour to each other - time and events conspired to ensure they hadn't met until after he had got married and had a child - he was too young to get married - it was a forced marriage - his wife was an abusive alcoholic - 'If only we had met before you met her it would have been us, and only us'. Of course what would have happened if he hadn't met his wife never occurs to them – the circumstances required for the eventuality of their meeting would never have arisen.

Those furtive days at the beginning of their entanglement were, in many respects, the most exciting. Obviously, they were completely professional within the workplace in such a way that no-one would ever suspect their romantic coupling outside the confines of the office. However, because he had to return home by 5.30pm each evening (to avoid a suspicious wife) they developed increasingly clandestine ways to be together - an afternoon meeting with clients which finished earlier than expected - an early morning networking event no-one would check up on....

She remained his supervisor for five years until, by a quirk of fate and the chauvinistic attitude of the firm's partners, he was promoted above her to become head of department and, by default, her boss. It was only then that suspicion of their secret relationship started to arise in the minds of their colleagues, especially when he promoted her to be his deputy and moved her into the office next to his. Nevertheless, they were oblivious to the gossip and the reality they had become the main source of entertainment in an otherwise dull working environment.

During these years he ceased (or so he claimed) to have any intimate connection of a sexual nature with his wife - he had moved into the spare room on the pretext that the snoring brought on by her drinking habits prevented his sleep. The lover agreed he should not seek a divorce until his one and only son was old enough to leave home. She had met the wife a year before they commenced their affair and could see the logic of not 'rocking the boat' - the wife was of a jealous and fierce temperament. The lover was also worried the impact a divorce could have upon her own career prospects, especially within the rather conservative city of their residence.

It was fairly apparent to the most casual observers that the wife did not particularly like, trust, or care for the husband. Shortly after he had started to work for the city firm the wife engineered an evening 'dinner ' for her husband's colleagues during which she could size up the potential opposition and flirt outrageously with the men in order to embarrass, spite and belittle her husband. Although the evening was called a 'dinner ' it was basically a drinks party with a take away curry from the Taj Raj thrown in for good measure. It was at this 'dinner' she first met the wife.

That night in the semi-detached house in the suburbs of the overpopulated city, the wife had oozed sensuality from her skin in equal proportion to the excess alcohol leeching from the pores of her body. She wore a ridiculously short tight mini skirt with a low loose cut blouse, and chose, most intentionally, not to wear a bra to support her somewhat large pendulous bosoms. These she seemed particularly happy to display to any male who came within her vicinity by leaning forward and allowing her loose blouse to reveal their full glory crowned at their pinnacle with large pink nipples. The wife had obviously been very drunk and it was impossible not to notice that every time a man wanted to know where the toilet was she would lead him upstairs to find it.

The lover had met the wife, heard the voice, judged the behaviour and instantly felt pity for the poor husband who was obviously living a life of unadulterated hell. The sexual innuendo started shortly after the 'dinner' when the husband arrived at work looking harassed and upset. With a little gentle coaxing he told her that the previous night his wife, in a drunken state, had, in front of their son, accused him of having an affair with her – his boss. Later she had got so drunk she urinated through her clothes onto the settee and collapsed onto the floor. He had carried her upstairs to bed. The child had been looking from the landing as if watching a play – just staring at the scene as it was playing out. He shouted at the child who silently turned away and went into his bedroom. The husband was obviously feeling guilty for something he hadn't done – yet.

She starts teasing him about his wife's outrageous allegations, just innocent little comments such as" – so lover boy what does she think we'll be doing today?" - delivered with a wink and a smile as she hands him the morning work schedule. Naturally, he was rather taken with the attention being directed towards him by this slightly older woman who just happened to be his boss, and became increasingly aware of how attractive she was. She, in her turn, couldn't help but notice his attraction and was equally flattered by the attention paid her by this quite good looking younger man. The journey from innuendo to outright flirting was inevitable - "I think you will find these case papers sufficiently arousing or maybe you could do with a little more stimulation in your life?" - delivered with a knowing smile as her fingers 'accidentally' caresses his as she hands him the file. Eventually she persuades him, on the pretext her car had broken down, to take her home that one afternoon to collect some intentionally forgotten files.

It was ten years later when both she and the wife discover he is having an affair with a young secretary at the office. She hadn't a clue it was going on, but it was, underneath her very nose, and, just to add salt to her wounded pride, whilst she was still having an affair with him.

He would never be able to justify his behaviour - certainly he didn't enjoy living the duplicitous life it had created for him. In his own mind, he wasn't in control, it just happened - he was given no choice, circumstance pressed the start button and he had no idea where the pause or stop button was.

As indicated previously, it is often considered that most people engage with their little affairs in order to obtain the validation required to justify their own existence, a validation their existing sexual partner can no longer give them whilst they are desperately seeking their own. This may well have been the case for him, however, all he actually attained was an understanding that no romantic affair concludes with the 'happily ever after' idyl meandering into the sunset - inevitably they climax in the anger and bitterness of a cold grey autumn morning, shared equally between all parties concerned.

Both the lover and the wife are united in the disavowal of the husband. The wife divorces him citing the affair with the secretary. The young secretary is made redundant. The betrayed lover, considering her position as his deputy untenable, sees no alternative but to hand in her notice and seek employment with the company's main competitor. She applies for a role, and, within this somewhat more enlightened firm, is taken on as a senior partner.

In the aftermath of her 'disappointment' she re-engages in the world, 'sans lover', with a degree of relief and abandon she finds truly liberating. In her spare time she develops a taste for athletics, sailing and computer dating - the latter arising from a difficulty in finding a suitable boyfriend 'to scratch an itch' within her immediate sphere of influence - she certainly has no intention of romancing with a work colleague ever again. Computer dating seemed to offer the suitable answer to this dilemma and she rather enjoyed the allure of creating her somewhat gregarious and mischievous online persona. She fondly considers this period as the time she went 'off the rails 'and lived dangerously – in reality she barely left the station. Whilst she dreamt of being swept off her feet and making love to some glamorous youthful adonis, she was not likely to be aroused by any of the few rather dodgy individuals she met online. Within less than a year she gave up on the online dating game following a close encounter of the seedy kind. From then on she focussed solely on her work and athletic hobbies.

The lovers' path crosses four years later at an international accountancy conference. In the intervening years they had had no contact, and, somewhat surprisingly, had never bumped into one another prior to the catching of each other's eye in the conference hotel lobby. It is love with second sight. The three nights they share together are liberating, an excising of the past guilt that neither had realised they were feeling. He had matured, was single, and lived in an apartment in the centre of the city, not far from the offices of the firm where they once both worked.

They carry on as though they had never fallen away - as if the intervening four years had not existed. They agree never to discuss the content of their gap years - for some secrets are best left, hidden away from the prying eyes of lovers - and, despite being a definitive and recognisable 'item', seem dis-inclined to get married or move in together. They ignore the accepted social mores dictating what 'real couples' should or shouldn't do and continue living' separately 'in their respective homes.

They maintain their independent professional lives, working in direct competition to each other during the daytime. They maintain strict boundaries with regard to their work life -never again will it be allowed to play a part within their relationship - it is a private endeavour in which the other no longer has a role - there is nothing to be discussed.

It is the evenings, weekends, and holidays that dutifully provide the sanctuary in which they become together. Within this refuge, away from the daily stresses of office life, they either choose to spend some private time in one or the other's place of residence, or go out for a meal - they are regularly seen out and about in the city's various restaurants. The majority of their holidays are spent overseas - they aim to visit three different continents every year. All in all they spend around sixty five percent of their free time together. The remainder of their free time is given up in recognition of the need to rest regularly within their own personal space - this is when she allows herself to focus on her hobbies - sailing and athletics, and he can focus on his one solitary past time - exploring different ways in which to breed money out of money.

The years pass as they always do with the one year merging into the next with ever increasing rapidity. They continue to live their life with the self-satisfaction that generally arises from recognising all is 'ok'. Of course there are times when they feel less than 'ok', however, on those very rare occasions they console themselves with the self-satisfaction of knowing there are plenty of people living around them with much lower levels of 'ok'-ness. She continues to convince herself that she loves him dearly and so is willing to play out the role of dutiful wife when required. He can't imagine being able to live a sensible life without her and so obliges in nurturing the role of caring husband as and when her need arises.

His obsession with breeding money out of money had developed slowly, sparked by an interest in what was happening to the personal pension fund he had set up with a reputable firm of investment managers. As he watched his pension pot grow at a rate unachievable through the average savings account, and considerably higher than the existing inflation rate, a thought trickled into his mind; he would take individual responsibility for managing his personal investments and create his very own portfolio. It couldn't be that difficult and it would save him money in the long run – he knew he had the financial acumen to achieve more than his advisers could. The call of the sirens was too much to withstand and although he didn't know it at the time, he was doomed to drown in the turbulent seas of his own personal financial meltdown.

The market he plays with is the wayward child of its human creators and benefactors. Like most wayward children it has come to the conclusion that it has matured independently from its parents, is more intelligent and wiser in the ways of the world than they, and can operate more than capably on its own volition within the very laws of cause and effect the parents believe only they can control. This particular child has no ill feelings towards the progeniturs, or indeed any people who choose to 'hang around' within the confines of its own personal play room - the child, without any prejudice or malice, will merely eliminate or elevate the players according to the prevailing whim of its own algorithm. For every winner in the game there has to be a loser. Today's successful buyer will always need today's unsuccessful seller in order to deliver the profit both players believe their actions will achieve - for every person who thinks it is a time to sell, another, hopefully, believes it is a time to buy.

Of course if everyone played with the same level of skill there would be no winners and no losers – everything would always balance out. This is the reality the professional gamblers hide within a complex language of TLA incapable of being interpreted by anyone other than those initiated fully within the child's game. Naturally, the professional addicts will make frequent wins, and of course, in order to maintain equilibrium, they will be made at the cost of the amateur addicts, of which he is one.

Addiction, resulting from the complex interactions of various systems of neurotransmitters, such as serotonin, dopamine, endogenous opioids and hormones, are responsible for creating the state where the human organism engages in a compulsive behaviour even when it is obvious that the very behaviour engaged in could have a significant negative impact on that particular organism's very existence.

The addict suffered from beginner's luck where for several years he did indeed make substantial profits from his investments. These early successes were of such significance that a luxury cruise down the Nile was arranged and paid for. The excitement and pleasurable feelings generated from the temporary increase in his personal dopamine levels from 'winning 'together with a possible problem with low levels of serotonin in the brain, encouraged him to spend more and more time 'playing 'the market. Finally the daily anticipation of 'playing 'the market started to generate as much excitement as the activity itself.

The initial success was not to be replicated. The more he 'played 'with the market the less success he had. He still made some gains but these were now punctuated by inconvenient losses. For several more years he operated at a profit but not one that justified the time and effort he was spending on his 'hobby'. The issue with his addiction only came to a head just prior to her sixtieth birthday.

Within the absorption of her very own compulsive need for athletic prowess and physical fitness, she had remained relatively oblivious to the amount of time he spent obsessing over the stocks, bonds and commodities he was dealing in. In many respects she was pleased that he had found such a productive way to use his time, especially as it had resulted in a couple of rather enjoyable holidays. Although an accountant herself she had no particular interest in the financial markets, she was more than happy staying within the specialist field of regulatory audit. Consequently she felt no difficulty in handing over a substantial amount of her savings for him to invest for their future old age. The initial goal was to invest the money and then, on her sixtieth birthday or thereabouts, draw down funds boosted by the inevitable profits he would achieve, spend a nice lump sum on a holiday, and use the rest to buy an annuity that would provide her with a fixed income pension for the rest of her life.

As her birthday approached she couldn't fail to observe that her long term partner was becoming increasingly anxious and showing signs of irritability. He was losing his temper and displaying a distinct lack of tolerance over the smallest of issues. He stormed out of a supermarket because the queue was too long. He shouted at a mother whose baby was being 'too noisy and lacking control'. He stopped his car in the middle of the road to argue with a driver who he claimed was getting too close to him. Everything and everyone was 'out to get him'. She questioned him about it. He had appeared sheepish, apologised and made some vague comments about difficulties at work.

As her retirement approached he bought the dream holiday they had been waiting for, a three-week break in Mauritius.

The holiday was not a great success. It became apparent from the very first day that he was not enjoying himself and seemed determined not to let her enjoy herself. He constantly remarked how expensive everything was. He didn't want to go out for dinner. He only wanted to buy cheap snacks for lunch. He argued over the price of wine. He refused to buy cocktails. He didn't want to pay for any activities such as sailing, snorkelling and other water sports. By the end of the first week she felt she was holidaying on her own. Every morning she would leave him sat in the hotel lobby with his head firmly stuck in the business pages of any English language paper he could find, and every evening she would return to find him sat virtually in the same position.

Naturally she tried to determine what was wrong but he wouldn't articulate anything of any sense. He seemed to believe his behaviour was normal and that she was the one with the problem. In the end she concluded it was all probably to do with their age and that her forthcoming retirement was a reminder he too would shortly be moving into a different phase of life. He had always enjoyed his work and was completely identified with what he did. His self-image was intrinsically tied his job title - an umbilical he was unwilling to sever - it supplied the validation he required to feel he was approved and accepted by the society he served. In short he was the typical product of The Boarding School. In his mind, if you took his job away he was a nobody, and it was true that the prospect of his retirement did worry him, so he did nothing to negate the rationale of her thesis. Unfortunately, his retirement in several years was not the problem he was having to address during this particular moment.

He only began to relax and cheer up as the end date to the holiday approached. The sense of his relief as he got on the plane was palpable. He was suddenly his 'old self 'again. However, this state of contentment did not last for very long. Five hours into the flight he started sweating profusely and feeling faint. The full seriousness of his situation only became apparent as they were due to land. The flight had been long so it was probably just as well that the acute myocardial infarction only took hold thirty minutes before their arrival back in the United Kingdom. They were greeted at the airport by an ambulance and it was on the journey to the hospital that he had the stroke, followed by another myocardial infarction. Then as now she had stayed at his bedside in the hospital throughout this first long illness. She stroked his feet and released as much of her own life force as she could muster in order to save his life – which she did. It was only when he was finally allowed home she discovered he had lost a significant percentage of her life savings, and most of his, through a series of very unfortunate investment decisions. She forgave him immediately.

He was forced to retire and she was forced to return to work. He now suffered from a whole range of disabilities brought on by both the myocardial infarctions and the ischaemic stroke. These grew steadily worse as the years passed and by the time he reached his early seventies he required constant care and support. Whilst they still lived in separate residences she nevertheless chose to take on the majority of his care needs after she finally retired. She promised him she would do so and he made her promise to tell him when it was all becoming too much.

She grips his hand.

"Oh you were such a stupid man, why on earth do I love you so much. Why couldn't we have had children? What stopped us?" She looks at the picture of his son and the grandchildren, and smiles.

She turns away from the photograph and into the face of the man she has dedicated her life to for so many years. She loosens the grip on his hand and starts to gently stroke his forearm.

It is at four fifteen pm when the consultant, with the duty nurses in tow, knocks on the door as part of his evening round. As they enter the room the lover acknowledges the consultant with a smile, gets up from her seat and goes out of the room - she believes the medical team should be able to undertake their duties without being scrutinised. She also feels the need to show her partner a degree of respect and not peer on as they clean him, empty the urine bag, and adjust his catheter. Instead she uses the rest period, which occurs at roughly the same point of each day, as a space in which to engage and connect with some of the fellow inmates and any concerned compatriots who may be visiting them.

This ward, as with all other hospital wards, has a continually evolving social community, which although only existing within any current form for less than a few hours, relies on gossip and stories for sustenance. There is always some anecdote to be shared which will lighten up the seriousness of any situation – mister ex civil servant has tried to get into bed with miss ex college lecturer on the grounds that it is only right for a husband to sleep with his wife - unfortunately she doesn't remember ever meeting him, let alone getting married to him. Someone else will have tried to escape, whilst another will have set off the fire alarms by trying to have an illicit cigarette in the bathroom.

She always leaves a moment as a gift for anyone. She either stops to say hello to those who indicate a desire to be engaged in pleasantries; or acknowledges with a smile, eye contact and the nod of the head, the others who she instinctively knows wish to remain with their loved ones undisturbed within the presence of their own thoughts. The nursing staff have started treating her as one of their own, part of the family so to speak. She has been in the ward every day for the last fourteen, ever since they brought him in with a urinary infection. Within a matter of days it had become apparent there was something more seriously impacting his life force. As a long term visitor she had caused no concern whatsoever; she had been courteous and showed great respect to all those who worked and cared for him.

Around fifteen minutes later she returns to the room. The nurses are still making the bed and trying to make the occupant more comfortable. The consultant is updating the case notes. He turns around as he hears her come through the door and seeing her, places the notes back in their residing place at the end of the bed and takes her hand in his.

Such acts of familiarity are not generally the norm; however, they have known each other for some eight years now, both having a keen interest in the health and well-being of the patient lying on the bed. The consultant is fond of this woman - she is graceful and he admires the love and care she not only shares with the invalid, but with all the others who come within her sphere of influence.

"I have increased the input level of intravenous morphine to ensure he is not feeling any significant pain. I have to tell you that in my opinion we are talking hours not days. However, I recall saying something like that once before and he was up and walking in three days"

She looks into the eyes of the consultant and registers the sympathy and concern residing within their depths.

"Thank you for being so open with me – would it be an idea to ask his son to come over now. He was going to come tomorrow but if you think it will only be hours. Are we at that point?"

"Yes, I believe we are. I think it would be advisable to give his son the opportunity of coming over now. Is there anything you would like me to do for you?"

"Yes, would you mind asking the duty chaplain to come over? In his own way he was quite a religious man and his parents were extremely devout – I think it would be appropriate for him to receive the last rites."

It is around forty minutes later when she hears a knock on the door. She looks over to the door and watches the duty chaplain enter quietly.

The lover is somewhat surprised to see a young woman, in her late thirties, with long red hair cascading over slight shoulders and falling just short of her waist. She is wearing a multi coloured skirt and jacket covering a plain pink clerical shirt with dog collar, the colour of which matches her boots. A salmon coloured pashmina has been arranged over her shoulders and allowed to fall down the front of the body as if it were liturgical stole. Around her neck is an ornate black cross set on a six pointed golden star surrounded with a silver circle. The chaplain registers the lover's look of surprise and smiles.

"Father James is not on duty tonight, he has gone off to a conference - he asked me to stand in for him over the next couple of days if the need arose. I am quite new to the area. I took up the resident post of pastor for the Church of Universal Values six months ago." She looks over at the resident of the bed. "I understand he is dying would you like me to pray with you?"

"Yes that would be nice, would you mind reading him the last rites?" She looks at the chaplain curiously - she has the sudden feeling it is highly unlikely this young girl will be able to fulfil this request.

The chaplain moves to the side of the bed, makes the sign of the cross using the trinitarian formula, places a hand on the shoulder of the sick man, and without hesitation starts reciting the liturgy associated with the visitation of the sick, exactly as it appears on the pages of the sixteen sixty two book of common prayer. However, she is reciting it from memory, expressing the words within a beautiful lilting voice more akin to music than speech. The lady by the side of the bed is transported to another time and space. When she becomes aware of the silence following the conclusion of the liturgy she finds there are tears pouring down the side of her cheeks. She can sense the chaplain's hands on her shoulders.

Finally she manages to find her voice.

"That was truly beautiful. Thank you so much. I am sure he would have felt your words."

The chaplain looks at the lover - there is a strange look in her eyes which the lover doesn't acknowledge or recognise.

"Would you mind if I recited a passage - it means a great deal to me personally and I believe it is appropriate for this particular time."

The lover nods her approval. The chaplain joins her hands in prayer and gazes upwards as if connecting to some higher source than her own. With the same musical lilt in her voice she begins her incantation from the Gospel of St. John, Chapter 15.

"I am the true vine, and my Father is the gardener. He cuts off every branch in me that bears no fruit, while every branch that does bear fruit he prunes so that it will be even more fruitful. You are already clean because of the word I have spoken to you. Remain in me, as I also remain in you. No branch can bear fruit by itself; it must remain in the vine. Neither can you bear fruit unless you remain in me. I am the vine; you are the branches. If you remain in me and I in you, you will bear much fruit; apart from me you can do nothing. If you do not remain in me, you are like a branch that is thrown away and withers; such branches are picked up, thrown into the fire and burned. If you remain in me and my words remain in you, ask whatever you wish, and it will be done for you. This is to my Father's glory, that you bear much fruit, showing yourselves to be my disciples.

As the Father has loved me, so have I loved you. Now remain in my love....."

The chaplain stands silently for the moment and offers a blessing before leaving the room with a promise to call in later that evening.   She suddenly feels both old and extremely tired. She wants a rest, a space for herself and her life. She turns to the man lying in the bed, takes his hand, strokes it gently, and speaks to him in a very quiet and calm voice.

"You asked me to tell you when I couldn't go on with this anymore – when I couldn't cope – when it was time to let you go. Darling, I love you very much and the time has arrived when we have to part from each other's company temporarily. It is time to go."

He opens his eyes for one last time and she perceives the slightest acknowledgement through the pressure of a finger.

They believe the lover died at around seven thirty. The son discovered her slumped in the chair next to his father who was lying in the bed fast asleep, gently snoring and breathing normally.

# Conclusion – Understanding the Vine

'The truth of your belief is only limited by your imagination'

So have you been touched in any way by these little stories of ours? Do they remind you of certain aspects of your own personal experience of life? Do you feel that you understand the nature of the vine and how to fight the contagion that surrounds it? Do you feel you have found an answer within our tales? If you have – congratulations. However we would cautiously advise that although you may feel you have found the answer, it is extremely unlikely.

Alternatively you may think there is no answer to find – these are stories after all. It is possible that you may contemplate that as such they have nothing to do with you and the pleasures of living in this world. However, we would then ask you to contemplate why we chose to tell you about these particularly insignificant people? Are you not interested to find out what happens to them and why they are inseparably linked to you as well?

We have found our voice and we have much to tell you, however, from here on the decision to listen is yours. We will be watching and observing you as always. Just give us the Sign.

## About Paul Ogden

Paul is a musician, writer, composer. The Insidious Vine is his first novel and the first part of a trilogy. He has also recorded The Insidious Vine as an audio album with a complete music score. This will be available shortly. For more information or if you have any questions about the book contact Paul by email at paul@somaholis.co.uk

See also www.theinsidiousvine.com